BLESSING IN DISGUISE

Dr. Sripali Vaiamon

iUniverse, Inc.
Bloomington

Blessing in disguise

iUniverse books may be ordered through booksellers or by contacting:

iUniverse
1663 Liberty Drive
Bloomington, IN 47403
www.iuniverse.com
1-800-Authors (1-800-288-4677)

ISBN: 978-1-4697-3233-6 (sc)
ISBN: 978-1-4697-3234-3 (e)

Printed in the United States of America

iUniverse rev. date: 1/28/2012

Preamble

BLESSING IN DISGUISE is a novel based on certain characters of the Indian Epic Ramayana supposed to have been incarnated in this century with completely a different outlook. They will be revealed at the end of the story which has been blended with reality and fiction. This is actually a satirical fantasy where there is no resemblance to any genuine person, character or incidence.

Dr. Guptha, a renowned Gynaecologist in Canada who excels in embryo therapy where he could ameliorate maladjustments such as clubfoots, hole in the heart etc. prior to the birth. He is also an owner of a winery in Niagara and an orchard in Brampton. He is involved in a research to extract information in a human brain by means of quantum and super computers. His daughter, Sitha is a dancer excels in western and Indian dancing and was reading for the doctorate on Archaeology at the Peradeniya University in Sri Lanka. She is staying at the bungalow of the Minister of Religious Interests, who is involved in building an International Religious Complex with the Replicas of famous Religious places in the world.

His wife, Dorothy visited Dr. Guptha's family in Canada with the Minister's body guard, Faizal who is in love with his batch mate Sub- Inspector, Kumari. Kumari didn't want to get married to him as he is a Muslim but desired to keep him as an eternal boy friend. Dorothy on her way from Canada visited Khajuraho in India where there are hundreds of erotic sculptures along with Hindu and Jaina temples. She got an inspiration to build a mini-Khajuraho in Sri Lanka with video clips on sexology for the benefit of married people. She also was involved in drug trafficking with a Muslim business man, Iqbal and was caught by the police when she was in disguise. She adopted a lunacy and got admitted to Lunatic asylum. But home people were not aware. They searched all over but everything was futile. Meanwhile, her sister's daughter, Mangala was involved in a rag incident in the University, where a girl, Ursula supposed to have pushed down from an upper floor and her spinal cord was affected. Her father was berating and trying to shoot at Mangala but Sitha secretly sent her to her parents in Canada. There was a dead body of a middle-age woman in a nearby jungle. Minister and Faizal suspected Ursula's father must have killed Dorothy and dumped in the jungle. They went with a police team and their bionic bitch. Head and the part of the body have been devoured by wild animals and the rest was almost decomposed. Minister identified the body as his wife, brought home and had the cremation. On this bereavement all were upset and Faizal decided to marry Sitha as their chemistry seems to be compatible and informed Kumari. She got a shock and was desperate, plunged into a murderous mind to destroy Sitha. She invited both of them for a dinner prior to the wedding day. While they were returning home she followed by her parent's old Humber. Slammed behind at the precipice of Kadugannawa. Their car tossed up and has fallen down to the valley. Her car also skipped off and fell down with a blaze. Sitha's leg was broken and was taken to Canada. It was amputated and later she was able to dance with a prosthetic leg. Kumari was badly disfigured with burns but she had a Mantara of Ravana given by an Upasaka with which she could stay invisible. The story is stunning, potent, powerful, and continues keeping the avid reader in suspense.

Contents

Chapter 1
Dr. Guptha's Arrival from Canada

"Doctor, do you believe a man can give birth to an offspring?"

"Well! God did not create man for that purpose. It is the birthright of women to bear children. What made you ask that curious question Dorothy?"

Dr. Indrajit Das Guptha, the only Indian gynecologist attached to Brampton Civil Hospital in Canada, who has earned a huge name for his magnetic embryo therapy with which if he gets the opportunity in time could be rectified and corrected deficiencies, deformations and maladjustments such as club foot, hole in the heart, default limbs etc. prior to the birth. However he is scared to touch Siamese twins while in the womb. He is the most sought after gynecologist in Canada. He arrived in Sri Lanka on an invitation made by the Apollo Hospital to investigate the embryo of a pregnant mother of a wealthy Casino owner in the Island. At the same time he had been assigned to check nine other pregnant women who had already registered in the hospital. He was picked up by Dorothy Senanayake, the wife of the Honourable Minister of Religious Interests, at the Bandaranayake Airport on Friday morning and he was to be taken to Hilton Hotel, Colombo in the latest Mercedes Benz, the new C-Class sedan, awarded to the Minister by the President as an additional official car. She has got down 85 vehicles and generously awarded this luxury car to the Minister. Mrs. Senanayake was eager to use this for her personal requirements as minister prefers to use his old Benz. On the very first day she used to pick up one of their family friends, Doctor Indrajith Das Gupta who was known to the Minister from the time that he was learning with him in the Bangalore University, India. This is doctor's third trip to Sri Lanka after migrating to Canada and becoming a renowned gynecologist in the Brampton Civil Hospital.

"One of our known D.I.G.s- Deputy Inspector General of Police told me yesterday a queer incident. A woman of about thirty has given birth to a child, who had been conceived outside the uterus. Child has been taken by a caesarian operation and the mother and the child were in very good health .This of course has taken place about twenty years back. It was not a yarn and I believed what he demonstrated."

"Possibilities cannot be ruled out. But it is strange to be heard that the mother and child were in good health."

"That is what I heard. This had happened in a rural hospital down south where ultra modern facilities were not available."

"I do know three such cases have been documented. But in those cases either the child or the mother has died. Because it was so precarious! In this instance, if a doctor has detected in time he would have removed the fetus and terminate the pregnancy.

Indent must have grown in the abdominal cavity of the mother and the umbilical cord would have attached to outside of the uterus."

"What I got bewildered when I heard the news that the

doctor who performed the vertical caesarian has uttered, at this rate men can give birth to offspring."

"Perhaps...but I cannot totally agree at this time."

Car was stopped by two constables. One cop ordered the driver to get down and show the documents. Then he requested others to get down as he wanted to search the car. Madam Senanayake got furious. "Why the hell you want to examine my car. Do you know who I Am.?"

"I am not concerned madam! We are doing our duty."

"I am the wife of the Minister of Religious Interests. Who has given you this fanatic order? Wait I'll telephone I.G.P." She was telephoning with her cell. "I will send you to Angoda for this insult. I.G.P. I am Dorothy, the Minister of Religious Interests wife. I am travelling with a reputed Canadian doctor. One of your brats stopped my car and insulting me. He wants to search the car. Why on earth!"

I.G.P. asked to give the cell to the cop. "Here I.G.P. wants to speak to you." She handed over the cell to the cop.

"No Sir, No Sir, DIG David ordered me to check. Sir." (I.G.P. Inspector General of Police. He is the head of the Police Department.)

I.G.P. had asked the S.I. to apologize to her and allow her to go.

"So sorry, madam! So sorry!" and he asked the driver. "You may proceed."

"See doctor, these cop- buggers are so high handed, to stop the car of an honourable Minister. I'll get the IGP to transfer him to the war trodden area of the North."

"You said you want to send him to Angoda."

"Yes doctor, Mental Hospital is at Angoda. They always want to harass people and get bribes. That is the prime reason."

"Must get the higher- ups to punish him."

They arrived at Hilton. A senior officer of the management welcomed her and the guest and accompanied them to upstairs. A bellboy directed them to the room allocated for the guest.

Little while later they were having lunch together.

"About the information on that childbirth I am eager to learn little more details. Where is she living? Could it be possible to meet her?"
"Well doctor, I heard she is in up country. But I am not aware where about. I have to get in touch with the D.I.G. and ask for more details. Why I was so queer about this case doctor, her husband was an insurgent. He had been mercilessly tortured.

He was a sturdy young man, educated fellow. But no woman was willing to get married to him. There had been something unimaginable had happened. A queer thing! That insurgent used to say it seems that it was a blessing in disguise. That woman, who was a widow and got married to this guy.

That was the only child they got and they are so poor couldn't keep the head above water. Man's fingers in one hand had been chopped off and he was not in a position to do any work. I am eager to help them if I know where they are."

After lunch and a delicious desert doctor asked. "Now madam what would be our itinerary."
"Tonight you may come to our place for a chat with the Minister and have dinner."
"Has he got enough time to have a chat, being a minister?"

"Yeah! It is a problem. He has no time even to sleep with me."

"So you must have a substitute."

She had a laugh "Yeah, you can't expect a rich and playful woman like me to live in an arid zone."

"Now, shall we go to the room and relax."

"Yeah, doctor."

They got up and entered the room allocated for the doctor.

"What is that queer thing about that man?"

"That man doctor had been one of the deputy leaders of the second insurgent movement cropped up in Sri Lanka in 1983. He had studied with their leader in Lumumba University, Russia. The late Mr.Rohana Wijeweera. While he served in the insurgent movement, JVP, He had been captured by the army and detained in a war camp at Homagama. When he tried to escape with 150 other detainees he had been got caught by the army and had been tortured severely cutting flesh in the body, chopping off fingers in one hand, pounding genitals, and due to excruciatingly painful position he had fainted and got into a coma. Army had assumed that he is dead. They wanted to dispose his body and the truck that was transporting him had been collided with a rock, turned topsy- turvy and blown out. This fellow had been thrown off. One of the native physicians who was passing by had taken him and treated." The telephone rang.

"May be for you madam." Doctor said.

She lifts the receiver, "Finished just now ...Why do you want me to come immediately?...Okay." She slammed the receiver. There is an opening ceremony at a temple and he wants to accompany me. He has forgotten to tell me early. Well doctor I'll leave now. I'll send the car around seven, for you to come. Then I am off." She placed a kiss on the cheek and left in a hurry.

She went straight to meet her colleague, Mr.Iqbal. She handed over him a parcel, in return he gave her a beautiful hand bag, may be as a token. She thanked him and went home.

The Honourable Minister was at the foyer.

"I am already late Dorothy, don't waste time to change your dress. What you are wearing is more than sufficient."

"If I go like this it is bad for you not me. Give me ten minutes." She went in hurriedly and returned after fifteen minutes. The Minister's face was like a jungle fire but he didn't utter a word.

Although the meeting was over Minister arrived just in time to cut the ribbon and open the image house of a recently built temple in his electorate.

Dorothy Senanayake is from a very rich upcountry family. Eldest child of Mr.Bandu Mollamure and his beloved wife Kamala. Her grandparents were from an aristocratic family. Due to a family feud over her marriage to a low country business man she was ousted from the family. Her husband who was involved in toddy business in Negambo gave it up and started a liquor shop but it has to be closed down as some thugs have smashed the entire shop over a quarrel. Subsequently he got in to do politics. He possessed a fairly big house at the Temple Road in Negambo where the famous Angurukaramulla Temple is situated. It is a posh and prestigious area. Wife inherited a 500 acre coconut estate in Chilaw, near the sea coast plus further half of the wealth of her parents after their demise. Became the sole owner of several houses in Colombo. Consequently she became a rich woman. She is very good at art and sculpturing. Particularly painting of landscapes. She gets emotional satisfaction through paintings. At the Heywood, the art school; she was good at drawing live nude poses of both men and women. But was not so eager to pursue.

Dorothy who had her education at St.Bridget's Convent in Colombo 7 was boarded at her uncle's house in Barnes place, closer to former Prime Minister Bandaranayke's mansion. It was closer to the school too. Her parents had bought her a red colour Porsche.

After school she used this sports car to roam about with her friends in Colombo and she became a very playful woman. Didn't pay much attention to her studies. Perhaps, because she has a bountiful heritage. Consequently she was failed three times at G.C.E. (O level exam.) and decided to leave the school in order to look after her parents' properties as they are now no more. She was eager to become a philanthropist and used to help those who are needy with parents' money. She became a social woman. Friendly with lots of young boys of rich families in the capital, Colombo.

When her uncle realized she is wasting money and living a carefree life, he made a proposal to an elderly member of the parliament. She agreed as he is a member of the ruling party who endowed with some status although he is about 25 years older to her. After the marriage, couple settled down in his parental house in Negambo, which she refurbished, as a posh mansion.

"Dorothy I am getting a portfolio. But it is useless becoming a minister if you can't make sufficient money at least to spend on elections." Husband revealed while stepping down from the car at their portico.

"What do you mean?"

"Today after the Parliament session was over, when I was chatting at the lobby with some news paper reporters, President summoned me to her chamber and offered me the portfolio of the Minister for Religious Interests. I could not possibly ask for something else. So I agreed. What can you earn with such a portfolio? Can't possibly get even some commission from any quarter!"

"She knows you are a religious minded man. In all these religions, even queerest one, contain at least some hint of the truth. She is also well aware that you are a saint type quaint and home-spun simple man although you were a tavern owner sometimes back. But to earn money there are ways and means, Jack. Don't get disheartened. I believe in every problem there is a solution. You have to think deep. Without money absolutely useless to become a Minister in a country like Sri Lanka. Just think for a moment. Why she offered you a luxury car. She knows very well you are not a man anxious for luxury. Because she has got down a few dozens of cars just for the sake of commission. Getting commission is not an offence. It is not something coming under the Bribery act. She can't possibly use such an amount of vehicles.

That's why she gave you an additional car. So you also should think about ways and means to obtain commissions. I will give you the tips. Don't bother.

Here, each and everyone creep into the Parliament to make money rather than render a service to the country. Why don't you deliberate on a massive religious complex for all the major religions. Religions in any country will remain as a major human belief for another few centuries. Make an elaborate scheme and submit to the cabinet. They will never go against a religious matter. When you offer contracts to several high contractors you can get thumping commissions. Moreover if you make an attempt, in addition, to get religious donations from other countries, you can get underhand deductions from the amounts they donate. According to the present parliamentary administration you have to appoint me as your personal secretary and subsequently you can entrust me the functions to handle the FUND. I'll look into everything thereafter."

"Not a bad suggestion Dorothy. Allow me to think about it. However if you planned to obtain commissions, a bigger percentage should be allocated to the President."

"Okay. I'll do that. Mind you that I too need money for my charity works."

This plan got gradually worked out. Dorothy was sure to become the Secretary of the Minister and she decided in advance to open up a folder for the fund and take over the full authority to conduct everything legitimately even prior to the cabinet approval.

But she felt that alone is not sufficient for her to throw money on various social ventures and earn a name as a recognized philanthropist. She dispensed kindness, compassion and involved in good deeds to poise as a philanthropist.

So she didn't want to give up the connection she has with the drug dealer Iqbal, who used to get down contraband and drugs from Thailand. Dorothy has made arrangements to unload illicit goods at her property in Chilaw. She also had agreed to transport drugs wherever and whenever necessary by her husband's official car.

When her husband was granted the Portfolio, President generously offered him a Mercedes Benz as an additional official car.

The Minister is of course a simple and home-spun man and he is not so eager to go by the latest Mercedes Benz, instead he was often using his previous official car, Mercedes 180.Which he inherited from his father and made it the official car, so that maintenance, gas(gasoline) etc. would be free. Only if there is an official function in the electorate he uses new Mercedes Benz, as such other times Dorothy who likes immense luxury gets husband's brand new car for her personal use. There were two official drivers at home. One is permanently engaged on the requirements of the lady. He is a police cop and was aware with female boss's illicit affairs and he always safe guards her. He is fairly compensated for his loyalty.

The above was one of the instances where police stopped her car to be searched. Because of the Minister's name and the Minister's car she brilliantly escaped.

On the following day the Sub-inspector who was ordered to search her car, visited the lady's bungalow to apologize her personally.

He is a free lance, popular cricketer, Faizal Vibhisana Mohamud, a handsome youth. He is sturdy, bold, brave and resourceful. Height is 5 ft.7ins. There is a prominent cleft in his chin which poised a virtuous look.

Madame really admired the fellow and requested whether he is willing to serve her husband, the Minister of Religious Interests as the chief body guard. He enthusiastically agreed with the offer and then and there she discussed over the phone with the IGP who is friendlier with her than the Minister, to appoint him for the envisaged post.

IGP agreed to do it but he says he is a very clever chap to raid illicit joints and illegal contraband. So time to time DIG, Gampaha District may require his services. If your Minister could release him in such instances, he could be appointed.

Mrs. Senanayake agreed to fulfill that request. Thereafter IGP instructed Admin. to release him on that specific condition. From the following week he was appointed to the post. He was provided with a room in her bungalow to take lodging, and of course, food and other facilities were available to him free of charge. That was an added advantage. As a Sub Inspector he was entitled for an official car or a loan to purchase a car. But he did not ask for it.

Dorothy has a bionic pet bitch that of a cocker spaniel. When Dorothy asked one of her servant girls to show him the room, assigned to him, the bitch, Nelly also followed him and got on to the bed and asked him to sit. He got amazed as the bitch was able to talk.

"Thank you"

He sat and stroked the bitch.

"Well I am also a body guard, of the lady not that of the old, moribund Minister."

"You don't like him?"

"I hate old people who are living in the 19th century. I like my boss, madam. She is a nice lady. Very forward and optimistic."

"So you like the lady."

"Very much, no two words about it. Kind, compassionate and always on the move. Wherever she goes I go with her and protect her from every possible source. Whenever she leaves me at home and go I have no grudge. I stay behind and look after her room. Answer her telephone calls. I am quite loyal. But Minister is married to the parliament. He doesn't have that much of love to this good lady. Husbands must love their wives as they love their own bodies. But this man is quite indifferent. Although the madam is quite sensual and voluptuous! "

"Good that I came to know about all these. So that you too can help me wherever and whenever necessary?"

"I'll help you don't bother. So you assume duties from today?"

"No, from next Monday."

"Okay Sir! Then excuse me I have to go out and be at the foyer."

"Thank you."

"You are welcome."

Nelly left.

Faizal was extremely happy that he was getting a job at a respectable place rather than dealing with gangsters and criminals and always involve in the dreary activities of evil doers of the society. He immediately left the Minister's bungalow and on the way stopped his motorbike in a place where there were no hustle-bustle but a quiet place. He pulled out his cell phone from the shirt pocket, pressed the number of his batch mate, S.I. Kumari Amunugama, who is often working together. "Hi, what are you doing?"

"I just came to relax a bit Faizal, after writing that dirty report of the gangster, Gudu Marshal. I had a terrible feeling of nausea. I closed that damn thing and dumped in the drawer and came over to the flat to relax a bit. Where are you telephoning from?"

"Just off the Temple Road, Negambo. I told you in the morning that I am going to meet Madam Senanayake. So I came straightway from the office."

"So what happened?"

"It is Okay. I have to assume duties from Monday…"

"Oh baby!…"

"I'll come over to the flat to discuss further. Bye!"

He folded and kept the cell inside the shirt pocket and rode fast.

Within half an hour reached the Regal flat, where Kumari and Faizal had taken on rent a room for them to spend their leisure hours. Particularly Kumari doesn't want to hang around in free hours with Faizal in the Mess. So they decided to get this room on rent, where both share the rent. Moreover Kumari was studying guitar playing under Anton Perera, which she found it is difficult to do at the police quarters. She is a music lover who has an aptitude for pop music even at the time when she was at the University and Police training College. She can sing very well almost like Vicky Leandros-Come what may-fame. She sings Que Sera, Sera, Whatever will be, will be, as the original version by Doris Day.

Faizal parked the motor bike at the basement garage, removed his uniform jacket and cap, dumped in the luggage carrier and came up by the elevator, tapped at the Kumari's door. She immediately opened as she knew it ought to be Faizal. "What men! We are pruning the opportunity to meet each other." She put her hand around his waist and closed the door. She was not that happy but gave a light kiss on the cheek. There were pieces of water melon on a dish on the table. He ate a big chunk and sat on the bed.

"We can and we must find convenient times to meet each other. Kumari was cuddling him and repenting.

"If you are at that end, how can we meet so often. Where are you going to stay?"

"Probably at their bungalow.'

"There you are! You don't feel sorry when that I am lonely here in Colombo."

"Kumari we are Police officers. We have to serve where ever that we are posted." He gave a kiss on her forehead, got up and stripped off his shirt revealing a hairless broad chest and hang the shirt on the rack. She too got up hold him tight and placed her cheek on his shoulder.

"So what have you written in the report."

"Forget about it darling. These gangsters have no mercy at all even to an innocent young woman."

"You didn't reveal me the whole story."

"Minister of Education, Roland Silva has agreed to offer a teaching post to this young girl. But she doesn't have required qualification.

So he has prepared a bogus certificate then and there and given to her. Agreed to offer a higher salary. More than what others get in the particular category. He had asked her to sleep with her as his wife is away and children have gone to school. He got up, hold her hand and accompanied to the bed room. She has pleaded not to do anything. Parents have fixed her a wedding on the next month. He has told that won't be a problem and asked who the lucky guy is. What's the job he is doing? She has told he served as a security officer to a business joint close by.

"O, that's a very low job. I can appoint him as my secretary and offer a good salary." While speaking he has tried to undrape her sari. She totally refused and started trembling. He has pushed her to the bed. Then she had started crying loud. This guy has pressed and closed her mouth. When he was forcing she has got fainted. This bugger has raped that poor girl."

"These are very common things among politicians Kumari, not only here all over the world."

"But the dirty part is not that. He had asked one of his thugs, Kudu Marshal, who is an Al Capone type gangster, to kill her and dump somewhere.

He has brought her by his car and on the way she has regained consciousness.

He has taken her to an abandoned house which is probably known to him. Someone known to her has seen this and immediately informed her husband to be and the police. This boy has rushed by a bike and started interfering then Marshal has stabbed the fellow and try to rape this girl. She has hit him with a cross bar that was on the ground. He has got wild and stabbed on her back. Meanwhile with difficulty her boy got up and jumped over his body. This bugger had the knife in his hand with that he has cut him into pieces. Police has arrived. The fellow ran away from behind. As police know the guy they haven't pursue. DIG informed me to investigate. The knife has sunk about two inches in her body. It is a life threatening injury."

"Write a vague report. Don't you know these politicians?"

"That's why I am scared to write the truth. If this girl dies, I can write a bogus report."

"However don't write anything to reflect badly over the Minister. These politicians living with goons are real dangers to the society. They can do whatever they want and easily escape."

"You like to have a cup of tea?"

"Yeah! Although I am a police officer, I too have a sort of a giddiness when I heard your story. I too have a grudge with this rascal Kudu Marshal but nothing can be done so long as this government is in power. This bugger with his gang robbed my father's grocery stores sometimes back. Police taken them into the custody. But following day a minister interfered and has ordered O/IC to release the fellows. So they got away. As long as Ministers backing them I can't do anything! I have to wait until the government changed."

"Too much of sugar in your tea!"

"You have no diabetes, I can't prepare again."

"You know being a Police officer you must get familiar with all these gangsters who are getting ministers blessings. There was a hard thug by the name Jothi Upali. He has killed so many fellows. Once he has killed a goon of an opposition politician and cut off his hand and thrown over to the compound of politician's premises who was living closer to the Parliamentary building .When he tries to take up the matter in high level this goon has been appointed as the body guard of the Prime Minister. All these notorious gangsters who are drug dealers, abductors, kidnappers, plunderers and murderers are living with the blessing with political leaders. They who safeguard them. No government Officer could even talk against them.

Beddagane Sujeewa who killed so many people including a well known journalist became a personal Security Officer of the former Head of the State. There was a goon by the name of Abeypala, Mr. Wickramasinghe appointed him as the Chief Security Officer at the Katunayake Airport. There were so many goons in the company of political leaders. They survive because of them and enjoy a greater position than police officers.

Police Officers, even higher ups do not talk a word against them. If they do they will definitely get a transfer to an unknown job or to a remote region. Civil society cannot do a damn. Although there is gun violence in the country Government is quite silent. Ruling party does not take any action to seize the illegal weapons. Actually we are being police officers who are supposed to safeguard the civil society cannot do anything substantial. If we are to safeguard our positions, our posts, we have to adjust ourselves by studying well the movements of political leaders who are in power.

I am fed up with my job now."

"But what are you going to do? Escape to another country. Where ever you go the position is the same. That is the religion. That is the culture."

Kumari's cell phone rings. She immediately opened it up and answered. "No Sir, I have to write a report. Other than that nothing else…Okay Sir. I'll report immediately."

"DIG wants me. Are you coming with me?"

"No Kumari you proceed, I'll have a nap for half an hour and proceed to the Head Office. Leave the key on the table."

Kumari left. S.I. Faizal was dreaming about his new assignment but couldn't have a wink. He turned on the radio for local news.

"Since the changed of the Board, Minister of Sports proposed to appoint an Interim Committee to look into the mismanagement prevailing during the previous Board. Board appointed a fresh selective committee in view of the forth coming World Cup of 2011."

Faizal who is a freelance cricketer listened to the news with a huge interest. News reader further announced Kumar Sangakkara is likely to be appointed as the Captain of the cricket team as he has displayed a high standard during the past few matches played with the International teams."

Faizal considered whether it is worthwhile if he resigns from the police force and join as a permanent player in the Sri Lanka cricket team. Again he thought if he has to leave he may have to repay a big amount to the government because of the scholarship he had on training in Germany. Perhaps the new assignment he got would be trouble free and thought he can safeguard his position. He off the radio, put on his shirt, locked the room and went direct to the Head Office.

When S.I. Faizal reported for duty Dorothy introduced him to the Minister.
"Meet your second body guard, Mohamud, I told you. I.G.P. reluctantly released him."
"Ah good, from when are you suppose to assume duties?"
"From today Sir," Dorothy then left the room.
"What is your full name?"

"Faizal Vibhisana Mohamud, every one addresses me as Faizal."

"You are Muslim. Isn't it?"

"Yes Sir."

"How is that Vibhisana sandwiched into your name? It is a Sinhala name, rather Sanskrit?"

"Vibhisana must have been my name. When Father adopted me he has added other names."

Oh I see! You are an adopted son of Mr.Mohamud. How long you are in the Police Force?"

"Nearly two years Sir. I am a graduate in the Peradeniya University, had my advanced training in West Germany. I was attached to the IGP's Office."

"Good, then today when I am going to the office, you may accompany me. Let the other guard also come along with us."

"Okay Sir!"

I don't require so many body guards and Security guards to my house. I am not a criminal to get scared of anything-He told to himself.

Dr. Guptha telephoned from Hilton "Dorothy what time your beloved husband arrives home?"

"That man has no definite time doctor. I recently bought him a fairly big wrist watch, an expensive Rolex. But he has absolutely no time to look at it either."

"You must buy him a grandfather clock to hang on his neck."

"He will forget even that. He is a busy character. I told you, he has no time even to come and sleep with me."

"That's why you don't have children?"

"I don't want children from him! to become lethargic Tom fools. What time you are coming here I'll send the car."

"Around seven."

"Okay."

"Ask your friend, DIG also to attend. I have to discuss about the woman who gave birth outside the uterus."

"Okay. If he is free enough to come, I'll ask."

"Yes Dorothy. Please."

"Dorothy Senanayake invited Donald Gunaratna to come home for a friendly chat with the visiting Canadian Gynecologist.

Dorothy's bungalow had an early 20th century outlook and a sense of architecture where grandeur dominates. Now she has given a little bit of modern outlook. The front impressive garden highlighting a capitalistic appearance with two fairly wide iron gates and beautifully planned flower beds where mostly colorful roses and other vivid varieties are grown. It is an exuberantly beautiful garden. This colonial architectural house had two sections of rooms either side. The multi-peaked roofs thatched with Indian Calicut- tiles. At the front centre had a big portico where two cars could be easily parked. Foyer with ceramic tiles is also fairly big. Quite big enough to hold a conference. Minister always used to be seated on a big antique type lazy chair at the foyer. Whenever he sat there he used a big Manila cigar, which Dorothy didn't like much. So she always used to sit in the other corner where she won't get the smell of the cigar. They have number of servants, males and females at home, and a brilliant cook who makes very delicious dishes. Walls of the sitting and dining rooms are decorated with so many pictures drawn by M. Sarlis, famous artist for religious pictures. Back sides of these hanging pictures are the homes for innumerable pale brownish translucent lizards. At the central hall there are two elephant-tusks on engraved stands and enlarged photographs of the couple either side of the corners. In one side stands an antique-type Clarendon piano which she rarely touches. She didn't want to learn music during her school days but was crazy for painting.

A fabulous crystal fixture from past now hang in the splendid ceiling over the lengthy dining table. Master bed room is facing the dining room and it is easier to navigate through dining room to the master bed room. It's a six bed room- house. Three in each side. Separate places for servants, towards the kitchen. Behind the house from the interlocking brick patio a path cascades through flower beds to an open hut at the corner of the premises with a small gate facing the back road. Hut is being utilized very often for outsiders who come to meet the Minister and also to distribute food parcels on Sundays for the destitute people.

Dorothy is a philanthropist and she used to distribute hundred lunch parcels on Sundays to needy people in the area. A dwarf, Juwanis is in charge of controlling the crowd and do a fair distribution. Everyone address him for the convenience sake Juwa. Juwa's main job is to keep the garden clean and beautifully. Trim the grass regularly. He has to do the watering daily and fertilizing once a week. Mrs. Senanayake has an enormous love for flowers and to maintain a neat and tidy garden.

The D.I.G., Donald Gunaratna arrived prior to the doctor and was discussing about the transfer of the S.I. as the chief body guard of the Minister.

"This boy is an expert to raid illegal and illicit joints and very popular cricketer, serves time to time as a free-lancer in the main cricket team. So he may have to go on leave very often for practices and matches. Some times may have to go abroad. He would not be able to serve the minister always."

"However I like the fellow."

"If he is having a good physique, naturally you will like. I know that."

"Don't feel jealous man! He seems to be a nice guy. I didn't tell the Minister he is the Chief Body Guard."

"He is not a Muslim. Do you know that?"

"I thought he is a Muslim. But he also has a Sinhalese name, Vibishana. I was just wondering. He speaks very good Sinhala.

He is Donald Faizal Vibhisana Mohamud."

"What?"

"Yeah. His daddy is, Saffique Mohamud, a wholesale business -man, in Colombo."

"That I didn't know. Anyway that's immaterial. Only difference is he may have been circumcised."

" So what? Here comes the doctor."

Minister's car with doctor Guptha arrived. He got down with a beautiful satchel of wines.

"I brought you three bottles of typical ice wine from my Dasaratha winery in Niagara, Canada."

"Thank you Doctor. I like to see your Niagara winery and that beautiful Niagara Falls one day. I have been to so many countries, but still didn't get an opportunity to visit Canada."

"You are always welcome Dorothy. Any time you want to come, just get an overseas call. You have no difficulty to obtain visas."

"Not at all! Meet Mr. Donald Gunaratna, D.I.G. that I referred to."

" O! I am very please to meet you Mr.Gunaratna."

"Don't say Mr.Gunaratna, say Donald."

"I was very eager to meet you to discuss a very crucial matter interested to me." Doctor said very enthusiastically.

"Not only the woman even the man" Dorothy made a remark.

"Both are equally important to me from medical point of view and to meet them personally, learn more details."

"They are living in a remote village in the hill country, off Nuwara Eliya. We may require about six to seven hours to go there. If you like we can go tomorrow morning, early morning. At least by six we must depart from this area.

We have to be at Sitha Eliya before dusk. I am ready to go. No problem for me to obtain leave. I can make it an official leave. What's your idea Dorothy?"

"I will have to ask for a jeep from the Ministry.

It is bit too late. Anyway let me try."

She got up and went inside in order to telephone the ministry to request them to release a jeep.

Meanwhile doctor discuss little more details about the couple.

"When you said Sitha Eliya, it reminds me Ramayanaya. The Indian epic of Valmiki. Which I like very much. As a matter of fact I have named my winery and orchard as Dasaratha, the name of the Emperor in Kosala, Capital of Ayodhya, as given in Ramayana. "

"Yeah, yeah, doctor the legend has some connection to the area."

"Incidentally, my daughter's name also Sitha. One of the main characters in the epic. She got through BA and just set for MA and then desire to read for PhD on archaeology. She too would be interested if I convey this message to her."

"You would have come with her. In Sri Lanka there are abundant archaeological remains which are more than 2000 years old."

"Next time I'll come with her"

Dorothy came with the good news.

"Transport Division of our Ministry agreed to release a jeep and I requested to send it to the Hilton by 6 tomorrow morning and advised to pick up the doctor and D I G and come home to pick me up to proceed to Nuwara Eliya. I'll inform my bungalow keeper to prepare lunch for us."

"So you have made all the arrangements, and finalized everything so soon" Doctor exclaimed.

"O, it is so simple for Dorothy." Donald quips.

"Yeah, I'll inform the bungalow keeper. So that he will prepare lunch in time. She used her cell and telephoned the bungalow keeper at Nuwara Eliya "Simon. I am coming over there tomorrow for lunch with two other high ranked gentlemen. Prepare a special lunch and arrange rooms for them to relax."

He agreed. So gentlemen everything is ready. Nothing to worry!"

"Of course when you are here, we have nothing to worry." Donald is familiar with her activities.

"Incidentally Minister is not willing to accompany us?" Doctor asked.

"He will spoil our journey. Let him look after his ministerial affairs. Ah! Here comes a very good friend of ours. An archaeologist! He is the Commissioner of Archaeology. Well read man. Come, come, come Saman May I introduce, Dr. Indrajith Guptha, renowned Gynecologist in Canada. And of course you know our good friend DIG Donald Gunaratna. We are planning to go off Sitha Eliya to meet a known person." Dorothy described.

"Good that you are here. I am bit eager to discuss about that archaeological region, Sitha Eliya which is depicted in Ramayanaya, where we are planning to visit."

"Well doctor it is not an archeological region as such. Only the hamlet known as Sitha Eliya. There is a legend to say that Ravana kidnapped Sitha and brought by his air plane, Dandu Monara or Pushpaka to Lanka. She was kept in a cave as a captive in this locality. This is now known as Sitha Eliya. But we have not come across any such cave in the vicinity." Saman described while being seated at the conference table.

"But it is well illustrated that she was kept in a cave in that region In the Asoka forest."

"But the whole Ramayanaya is a legend. Although there are several names given to places in Lanka relevant to his story. Such as Wariya pola, means Airport, where he kept his aero plane, then Ravana Ella, Ravanagala, Ravana cave, Ravana Kotte, Ravanakanda, Sithawaka…etc. But we haven't come across any authentic artifacts or any such evidence to accept as historical."

"NASA has taken a photograph of Adam's Bridge or Rama Sethu, Adi Setu, or Sethu Mandir in between Sri Lanka and India, from Mannar in Sri Lanka and Rameswaram in India, where clearly show the bridge made of shale stones on the sea bed. This is an evidence of the authenticity of the story." Dr. Guptha revealed as he has a particular interest on Ramayanaya.

"Yes doctor, Ramayanaya is accepted as a legend. But still it seems that it has built up on certain authentic situations. Not throughout the story. As such some could believe it as a true story. Hindus have embodied certain religious values. They assume it as a religious epic."

"My opinion is although we called it a legend it could have been a true story. This story is well established in Thailand, Indonesia and Malaysia where they have depicted names, such as Ayodya appeared in Ramayana for their roads and several places. In Indonesia and Malaysia they performed this story for live audiences in the form of Shadow dances, which is known as Hayan kulit."

"Yeah doctor. However it has been categorized as a legend because it has combined with mythical beliefs and unbelievable occurrences."

"My daughter, Sitha Guptha, who is genuinely interested in archaeology. She had told me once that she is desired to come to Sri Lanka and search some of these places connected to Ramayanaya."

"Don't allow her to waste her precious time doctor. There is absolutely no such place identified by our archaeologists." Saman Prematunga revealed.

"When we go there tomorrow we could speak to our friends and inquire about this." Dorothy proposed.

"A friend of mine, on the contrary wanted to write this from the point of view of Sri Lanka as Ravanayanaya, giving a proper place to Ravana as he should be the prime character in the epic and he was supposed to be a king in this island which was then known as Lanka,"

"Well Mr. Donald, it is not a bad attempt. Hope he will look into those historical places in Sri Lanka relevant to the story."

"He will perhaps. There was a field officer by the name Gamini Punchihewa who has visited these places and written some accounts in one of his books. Wimal Abayasundara, a literary genius who undertook to write the book. We would be able to find some information if your daughter is interested. I can help you."

"Yes Dr.Prematunga. Please."

"Address me doctor as just Saman."

"Okay Saman."

"History is a vital concern of every intellectual."

"Yes, DIG. Archeology goes bit further. If she is interested on archaeology she would definitely desires to visit our archeological sites at Anuradhapura, Polonnaruwa and in various other places. Next time you come with her. I'll help her in every possible way."

"Thank you Saman."

"I thought doctor she is more interested on dancing" Dorothy interrupted.

"Yes Dorothy she excels in western and oriental dancing particularly that of Kathak, Manipuri, Bharatha natyam. But her professional area would be archaeology."

"You send her over here. I I'll look after her as a daughter of mine and make arrangement to visit areas that she likes" Dorothy proposed.

"To study archaeology profoundly she must get into a university in Sri Lanka. Canada is not a country where you find any historical places although some of the archaeologists have come across 4500 year old skeletal remains somewhere in the northern end of Vancouver Island and supposed to be that of Heiltsuk, the members of the first nation." Saman suggested.

"I'll discuss with her when I go back."

"It is a surprise! Here comes the minister, very early." Quipped Donald when Minister's vehicle arrived and halt at the portico. He got down and came in with his attaché case. "Give me few minutes. I'll have a quick wash and be right back." So saying minister went inside.

"He seems to be in a pretty good mood." Said the archaeologist.

"I gave him a colossal project. He has taken it up very highly. That may be the reason." Dorothy revealed and went in. Servant boy little while later brought a bottle of Chivas Regal and a bottle of wine. Another boy brought glasses and ice in a tray.

"Should we wait till the minister comes." Donald asked "All this time we were in a dry zone. Let's start." He opened up the bottle and others joined.

"I think the bottle of wine is for the minister" Saman had a doubt.

"No it is for Dorothy." They were discussing about the present day politics until Dorothy comes to discuss about the trip.

When minister arrived, D.I.G. got up as a mark of respect and earnestly asked,

"You don't like to join our trip to Sitha Eliya?"

"No Donald. I have a Board meeting tomorrow. At Sitha Eliya there is hardly anything to see."

"But we are on another mission" Doctor uttered.

"Ah, It's good for you. You can meet them and get more information. It is a very queer instance. But it would be very useful to you as a gynecologist. Well in my case, I have a very big project in hand. Today after a lengthy discussion with the President, on her personal approval I entrusted a Designer to prepare the ground plan.

So I am really happy. Once that is finalized I can put up a paper for cabinet approval. I will be fully occupied on this during the next few months. Dorothy is having a five-hundred acre coconut estate at Chilaw. I just want to push it for this purpose. A World Religious Centre. Would be able to get a considerable amount from the Government."

"You may have to cut down over thousand coconut trees. It won't be a congenial suggestion." Dorothy objected while Donald opened up the bottle of wine for her and pouring into the glass.

"I'll come with some papers to have a brief chat over this." He went in.

"That means minister is not in a position to join with us in any of our activities?" Donald uttered as the Minister was coming.

"Well well if there is anything paramount I have to find time for that."

"Have you arranged a comfortable vehicle with the Ministry?" Minister inquired while joining the discussion.

"I have made all the arrangements. Thank you."

"Incidentally Dorothy you have been appointed as my Personal Secretary with immediate effect. You will get a thumping salary plus all the privileges that I am entitled to."

"Thank you Jack."

"We must celebrate that."

"Of course! after our journey tomorrow."

"That's excellent. Now Honourable Sir, let us know something about your massive project." Donald proposed.

"Yeah just tell us the skeleton of the project." Guptha proposed.

"Well things are not yet finalized. It is going to be a massive project no doubt. What I envisaged is to build a religious complex with four massive shrines to four major religions in the world. Buddhism, Christianity, Islam and Hinduism. Provisions will be made for example, for Hinduism, separate shrines within the same premises for Vaisanavites and Saivaities. In Buddhism for Theravada and Mahayana, Islam for Sunni, the majority, then Shiite and Sufi, Muslims. For Christianity, Catholic and all the other major Denominations. Religions in the entire world likely to remain among the major human belief until the modern science will become full-fledged.

So there will have support from every quarter. In addition, there will have preaching halls, museums, lecture halls plus hotels and shopping complexes, exhibition halls etc. A multi-million project!"

"What about for Judaism, Sikhism and other minor religions?"

"Good that you remind me Doctor, I have to stipulate those in my plan."

"But don't forget that the whole suggestion came from me." Dorothy proudly said.

"So what do you want me to do? Put up a statue of yours?" Minister said while showing the rough sketch of the ground plan.

"I don't want such cheap publicity. I have different motives." They discussed in short much about minister's massive religious plan and pour some Scotch into their glasses.

They also chat on the political situation of the country as there would likely to be an election soon to elect a new President. The last term of the incumbent President is scheduled to be over in few months time.

Chef of the house played the gong and informed the dinner is ready.

"Take your glasses and let's go to the dinner table." Minister got up.

Their chef is a well experienced cook. Ranbanda. He had worked earlier at a hotel in Dubai. His wife Menika is a beautiful woman with a five year old child. She is pretty and trim enough to catch the eye of anyone. They are also from Balangoda. Dorothy's village. Quite loyal to Dorothy's parental family. Rambanda sometimes assigned to attend to affairs at Chilaw estate, particularly when plucking coconuts. When he goes there he stays one or two days. In his absence Menika look after the meals and kitchen activities.

They moved to the dinner table. Dorothy's cook had orchestrates a very posh table with a vast repertoire of dishes.

While enjoying Dorothy's delicious meal they all discussed further about Minister's massive project and the trip to Nuwara Eliya and from there to Katumana beyond Mahagasthota, where there is a narrow road leading to Hakgala National Reserve to meet this guy.

After the dinner Donald got up and said "Well tomorrow early morning we have to start our journey. Therefore it is high time to leave."

"Today is the only day that minister came home early." Dorothy said.

"Then you all can enjoy. We will take your leave." Donald, Dr Guptha and Dr. Premathunga bid them good bye.

"Dorothy I can drop the doctor at the Hilton. You need not send the car."

"Thank you so much Donald."

Dorothy's bionic bitch remained at the foyer until guests left the premises and she returned to the dining hall.

"Madam, am I to wake you up at six?"

"No Nelly. That's bit too late. Wake me up at 5.30."

"Okay."

"Without disturbing me please."

"I won't disturb you Sir, I know you are a man to sleep."

"I have plenty of planning to be done with regard to my project. I have to spend two three hours at night."

"No problem Sir. Allow lady to sleep comfortably. So that she can get up early. Thank you Sir. I am off."

Bitch went in to Madam's room with her.

CHAPTER 2
Trip to Nuwara Eliya

———————◇———————

Ministry of Religious Interests luxury jeep picked up the doctor Guptha and DIG Donald Gunaratna from the Hilton in Colombo and arrived at the ministerial palace in Negambo where Dorothy Senanayake was awaiting for them. She got in and servant boy brought madam's suitcase and kept inside the vehicle. They proceeded while Dorothy's bitch was eagerly waiting until they leave the premises. They went through Minuwangoda, Nittambuwa, Warakapola route.

When they reached Ambepussa in the Kandy road Donald asked. "Madam, we had only cups of tea in the morning, but no breakfast, I feel very hungry."

"Police officers and women are all alike. They are always in hungry, for something or other." Doctor remarked.

Dorothy ordered driver to take the jeep to the rest house. "Whenever we go to Nuwara Eliya via this way, we always have our breakfast here. Very courteous staff and food is excellent." Dorothy said while they were getting down the jeep.

"For ministers of course they always treat very well and offer the best of food." Donald said bit sarcastically.

"What about ministers' wives, they treat the same way."

"Very fortunate people in a country like Sri Lanka." Doctor uttered.

"Naturally, they are the best in the country elected by the people of the country." Dorothy quips.

"They treat the same way for police officers too."

"Naturally, they are the officers who protect the public." Doctor affirmed.

They entered the Rest House and seated in a cozy corner. While looking at the menu,

"Let's see, what we can order?" She went through the menu card.

"What do you like Donald?"

"Whatever you select and order we will consume, what do you say doctor."

"I agree with Donald."

She ordered various dishes although it was a breakfast?

"Why so much Dorothy? You may have to pay a big amount."

" No problem doctor. I can put it to minister's entertainment allowance."

"Some people have all the luck!" Doctor said.

After the meals thanked the staff and the Rest House keeper and left the place.

"We have a long way to go. Before dusk we must reach this fellow's hut off Katumana. In village areas people sleep very early. They can't afford to spend money on kerosene lamps." Donald commented.

Mrs. Senanayake said as she had asked her bungalow keeper at Nuwara Eliya to prepare lunch, after partaking lunch without wasting time we can proceed to their place via Katumana. They all agreed.

In a couple of hours' time they reached Nuwara Eliya and stopped the vehicle at the Minister's holiday bungalow.

Immediately after they arrived, Simon, the bungalow keeper came quickly and got madam's luggage. All of them got down and entered."

"O lovely bungalow!" Doctor uttered.

"If we can have a nap and go it is ideal."

"No time for a nap, Dorothy no harm having a wash so that you can refresh yourself."

"Yeah I must do." She went into her room.

Donald and doctor Guptha sat in the sitting room. "Doctor you like to have a tot before the lunch?"

"It's naturally a tradition."

Donald opened up the liquor cabinet and selected a bottle of whisky. "I think at this time a light stuff is better." He brought a Jonny Walker red label.

Simon rushed immediately and picked a bottle of soda from the fridge and brought it with the opener and glasses.

Donald opened the bottle of whisky and handed it over to Dr. Guptha. "I prefer with one or two cubes of ice instead of soda."

No sooner Simon heard what doctor said he brought ice cubes in a can.

"Dorothy you don't want an appetizer." Donald asked loudly. But there was no answer. Probably she must have gone to the wash room.

While they were sipping. Dorothy had a change and emerged out. "Why nothing for me?"

"That's why I asked. But there was no response. I thought you were sleeping.

"I had a body wash." She went to the liquor cabinet and brought a bottle of white wine. "Simon, get a glass for me."

He brought a wine glass and asked whether to serve the food.

"Yes Simon, do it." Dorothy said.

In about 10 minutes. Simon came over and said, "Lunch is ready madam."

"No time to waste, let's have the lunch and leave early." Donald said "Doctor is in a hurry to know how that woman gave an unusual birth!"

They all laugh and got up.

"Doctor, take one for the road."

Glasses in hand they went over to the dining room. They started serving themselves and although they were in a hurry they leisurely consumed meals while sipping their drinks.

After lunch they started their journey.

"I am planning to launch a very secret and an extremely essential discovery, with that nobody can hide anything. Everything will be exposed. Any secret of any human being, nothing can hide."

"Well, doctor that would be a marvelous discovery. We people need not waste much time on any investigation on any crime."

"Absolutely Donald, police and judges, even historians or archaeologists need not waste much of their energy or time to investigate on anything. Any secret of an individual could be traced within a second."

"But won't there be human rights infringement?" Donald asked.

"There would be! There would be. But those could be taken up separately. I have already installed a replica of a Super computer, Tianhe-1A model of China and Two quantum computers designed by IBM. Any way it will take fairly a long time to achieve my objectives."

"Then doctor what you want to know from this fellow the secret that you are eager to know you could easily find out from your computers?" Dorothy quipped.

"Absolutely! But I don't know how long I have to wait

to achieve the result of my project. I may have to get round computer wizards from other countries, India, China, Japan, America and other European countries. There are enough potential. I am dead sure about it. It would be a gigantic project. World could save billions once it is materialized."

They discussed at length what doctor envisaged from his massive experiment which he felt will take considerably a long time.

"We have come to Sitha Eliya." Donald looked around and said.

"Beautiful place! Could we look around a bit? Because of the name doctor had a particular interest."

"Yes, we can spend no more than half an hour." Donald said.

When they got down in Sitha Eliya they entered the Sitha Amman Kovil and spent nearly half hour. Doctor made donation and thereafter they had to proceed through a narrow road from Katumana and veered on to a bumpy path which took nearly two hours. At last they arrived at a bamboo and mud thatched hut at the corner of Hakgala Forest Reserve, where in the adjacent plot ex-insurgent Suraweera and his wife are living.

When Suraweera saw the DIG who is known to him came running and worshipped as he was worshipping a clergy.

"How are you young Man?"

"I am not young Sir, I am now past fifty."

"Fifty is nothing for a man like you," and Donald introduced Dorothy and Doctor to him. His wife also came out of the hut.

"We have no chairs to offer you madam and sirs. There is a bench under the tree. If you all don't mind."

They sat on the bench. Suraweera sat on the ground. Woman was standing.

They quarried about their personal well being and Dorothy asked "If you two are willing I can allow you to stay at my bungalow in Nuwara Eliya and attend to whatever the work available."

"That's a heavenly suggestion madam." Suraweera uttered.

"Only thing madam, we don't have proper clothes to wear in a place like that," Suraweera's wife was lamented.

"Don't bother I'll buy clothes and whatever you need. Where's your child by the way?" Dorothy asked.

"Child! No he must be a young man now about 22 years. I don't know where he is now." Suraweera said in a sad tone.

"Yes, he had told me the full story." Donald remarked. "As they couldn't bring him up had given to some childless couple in Colombo to be adopted." Donald further said.

"Instead of chatting here as it is about to dark shall we go with them to our bungalow in Nuwara Eliya?"

"That's a good suggestion Dorothy. Then you two get ready to go." Donald ordered.

"Sir, please give us ten minutes. We will have a wash and dress up soon."

"That's Okay." Donald said. They ran down with a bucket, perhaps to a water fall nearby for the wash. However within about 15 minutes they returned and were ready to leave.

When they arrived at the bungalow Dorothy introduced them to the bungalow keeper cum cook Simon, "They will attend to all your cooking, garden work or anything else that you ordered them to do. Allow them the rare room for them to stay."

"He agreed and directed them into a good room closer to the kitchen for them to stay. Both of them thanked all of them mouth fully and retired.

Simon had already prepared the dinner and came and requested what they need immediately.

"Donald said before the dinner it is the usual tradition to take a drink. If there is a bite it would be excellent."

"I have prepared fried wild boar."

"O! that is really marvelous! Simon."

Dorothy ordered Simon to bring a bottle of Whisky and a bottle of wine from the liquor cabinet, which he did quickly.

When he brought the bottles and glasses Doctor said he prefers to have some sausages or something like that.

"I too prefer sausages." Dorothy said.

Simon agreed to bring in five minutes and left hurriedly.

"Why don't we invite Suraweera also for a drink. He had been an insurgent he must be quite used to liquor." Doctor remarked.

"Why not! why not!" He asked Simon to call him. When he came he pulled a small chair,

sat behind them very punctiliously.

"Suraweera what do you like?"

"Anything is okay for me Sir."

You must be used to lot of hot things and Donald pours some whisky into a glass and offered, "You can have it on the rock." He thanked and took it. "I am of course used to Kassippu (illicit brew) Sir."

"You are being a graduate in the Lumumba university must have taken lot of Vodka. This is so light for you. Doesn't matter take it."

"I like to learn about your experience in the insurgency period" Doctor questioned.

"Yes you must be having plenty of things to talk about during that bravery period, of yours. "Doctor would be interested to hear about your wife's child birth and something else." Donald came out with amusedly.

"I can talk about my bravery and nasty experiences for days, Sir. But don't' know where to begin."

"You begin from where you tried to escape." Donald suggested.

"Well sir. In that case I can cut short and present the gist of it. It was during the second uprising of the JVP in 1987, I was one of the Deputy Leaders of the party. When we were in captivity in a dungeon house, at Homagama, near the Army camp, about 35 kilometers off Colombo, we were in the custody of army officers. We were not allowed to come out of the dungeon -house. We were about 150 captured insurgents.

Every day we were getting inhumanly treatments torturing, beating kicking and blackguarding. We were there for about two months. We were absolutely not aware what was happening in the outside world. I wanted somehow or other as a leader to take all our fellows out of this dungeon without undergoing daily tortures. I hit upon a plan. All agreed. We started digging a tunnel from an inside room where army fellows normally do not check. In about one month's time we were able to dig an L shape tunnel up to hundred meters with the help of some iron bars removed from a closed window. Which we presumed it leads to the adjacent jungle plot behind the barbed wire fence.

What I planned was nearly successful. We dumped all the earth collected from the tunnel in an adjacent room which was locked. One day, round about three in the morning one by one escaped. I was the last man. Army had smelled a rat. Two or three officers came out and used flash lights. They untied the army dogs. Two of them crept through the fence and followed the track and caught one of the escapees. At that time I was about to come out from the tunnel. They discovered the tunnel opening. I couldn't do anything else rather than returning to the cell. I crawled back hurriedly returned to my mat and covered myself fully and slept.

Army fellows who came over searching with flash lights and when they saw me faster asleep used filthy words and battered me inhumanly and dragged me into the torturing cell. They discovered all what we had done. They brought the captured fellow and started torturing. They didn't ask me a single question but allowed me to watch. It was not possible for me to watch Sir. I was dumbfounded. They were stretching his body on a ladder. Thereafter Suspending from both wrists and piercing finger nails with needles and giving electric shocks, dripping acids on his feet and constantly flogging by three fellows shouting with utter filth. He was screaming with pain but didn't utter a word.

They tried so hard to get information but miserably failed. Within one hour he was almost dead. He got fully unconscious. They then untied the fellow and dropped on the ground I think he was dead. Now it was my turn. My legs were tied with chains, both hands twisted back and tight to a pole."

For Dorothy it was either boring or painful to hear all the brutality and savaging descriptions. She got up and went away.

"Why Dorothy you are not interested to hear …"
"I am having a headache. I'll go and lie down for a few minutes and be right back for dinner."

Doctor said it is quite natural for a weak mind like that of a woman to hear all these horrifying stories and get dizziness. "Why not we wind up and go for dinner." Doctor proposed.
"I am more interesting to hear the other two subjects from Suraweera and his wife." Doctor indicated further.

"With Dorothy of course we can't listen to one subject but not the other."

"Well Donald what we can do if Dorothy is interested will think about some other strategy for her to listen. Let's discuss after dinner."

Little later they invited Dorothy and proceeded to the dinner table. Suraweera went down to the kitchen as he felt it is not fair for him to sit with them at the dinner table.

"About the child birth we have to ask not from Suraweera but from his wife." Dorothy proposed while sitting down along with the others.

"I don't think she could express, Suraweera will relate. He is a vociferous guy." Donald said.

"Madam, after the dinner you go to your bed room we shall provide you with a pair of earphone and we hide a mike in the office room, fixes it to the recording machine there. So that we could discuss everything openly at the office room without you. In your absence he has the liberty to express anything boldly and without hesitation. Whatever interested you may listen." Donald described.

Doctor said that is an ideal suggestion.

So they arranged accordingly and after about an hour when Suraweera and the others had their dinner Donald asked Suraweera to come to the office room.

They started the discussion. Donald was inquisitive to know how is that Suraweera got a long and sturdy tool. "Now continue Suraweera." Donald ordered.

"Well Sir, I was not tortured at the army camp. Two officers took me in blind fold, tightly hand cuffed and my legs and the neck were tied with a heavy chain. They took me by a closed jeep, to a torturing camp. Later I learnt it was Batalanda.

They put me into a room and locked the door. There were no windows in that room and ceiling was air-tight as such no possibility for outsiders to hear any sound. They removed my chains and later hand cuffs.

"Now you are free. Completely free! You must reveal everything, without hiding anything from us."

I didn't utter a word.

"Are you dumb or deaf?"

I kept my mouth shut.

"I know how to open your mouth." One guy removed my clothes and tied me to an iron crossbar fitted to two walls in the corner. There were only two officers.

The other guy hit my dangling balls with a baton. At first I resisted. Then he gave me a thundering blow to my stomach the other fellow also hit at my cheek. Blood oozed from the mouth. Uttering filth he battered my shoulders and untied me and brought near a table. Other chap then with his baton lifted my penis and kept on the edge of the table. "Your cock will be pounded like a thin razor blade unless you come out with the truth."

He yelled and said, "Tell in plain language. How you fellows dug the tunnel and escaped?"

I stammered slowly as there were no alternative "I didn't want to follow them Sir. That's why I stayed behind."

"You think we are damn fools to believe what you say." One guy gave me a baton charge again to my Tommy.

"No Sir, I am telling the truth. I too helped them to dug the tunnel. But I warned them not to proceed."

They uttered filth and asked, "Are you still trying to mislead us."

"No Sir. This is the exact truth, Sir." At that time one fellow broke a broom stick and tried to put in my ass. I worshiped them and agreed to tell them the exact truth. They wanted to treat me inhumanly to extract information. Before they do anything painful I wanted to tell the truth. Because I knew by that they won't gain anything. However I was confident that they won't believe whatever I say and moreover they were adamant to torture me. I started relating the exact story. While they were listening they opened up a bottle of arrack and started gobbling.

"Stop your damn lies you filthy bastard!" And gave a baton charge over my penis, but missed the target. Again he uttered filth and roared.

"Before getting bobit your rod. Tell us the damn truth."

"Well Sir, I am telling the truth. The Gospel truth! But I know you don't believe me Sir." I have absolutely no fear just for the death. But their cruelty in torture is deadly terrible. "Why don't you Sir, without torturing me further, hit with the baton to my head and kill me Sir?"

"To kill you!" He suddenly went on rigid with rage. "No! We don't allow you to escape from the death so easily."

He threats me by pointing the batten at me, "Don't provoke me further you devil. Tell the truth otherwise the baton will come over your cock pounding it like a shell of a cadju nut."

Before I uttered another word. Unexpectedly the other fellow pounded my penis with a mighty blow. I could remember only that. I got unconscious. Went into a coma.

These fellows may have thought that I am dead. They were fully drunk at that time. They may have taken my body and dumped into a jeep and have taken to dispose. It was dead at night and was raining heavily with thunder and lightning. I can't remember the time although by that time I was conscious. They drove the jeep in a terrific speed, may be because they were fully drunk. When they were speeding suddenly it got a jerk and dashed against a tree or a rock. I don't know where about. I can remember I was thrown out of the jeep and it burst into a flame and toppled down to a precipice.

Little while later a passerby vehicle stopped. Two people got down. One was an elderly person with a long white beard holding an umbrella. He asked me what happened and who I am. But I was not able to answer.

Because of the rain I was fully soaked with bear body and was shivering in the cold. Elderly person ordered the other man to take me into their vehicle. Later I found he is a famous physician. He had brought me to his house.

Adjacent to his walauwa type magnificent house there was a separate hut where he treats patients. They brought me over there and gave some clothes to wear and food to eat. Then one of his assistants brought a kasaya (medication) to drink. It was soothing and I inadvertently slept.

Following day Vedamahaththaya examined me and there were swells and bruises all over my body. He asked his assistant to apply some medicinal oil and then he noticed my penis has been pounded.

He ordered his assistant to prepare a medicinal plaster which he dictated by a Sanskrit Sloka. In about two hours time he brought it and under physician's supervision tight it to my penis, wrapped with a flexible bark of a plant and bandaged it.

That treatment was continued for more than two months. When it was finally removed only I saw it. I got astonished. It was longer and thicker than what it was. Then it was massaged with sweet smelling medicinal oil and due to stimulation it became thick and strong. Vedamahaththaya arrived looked at my penis and asked, "How young man?"

I blushed. He touched it pressed it, twisted and manipulated it in such a way it got a marvelous erection. He measured it with a foot ruler. It was 12 inches long. He said he is extremely happy by treating me he discovered a wonder drug. He had a huge smile and said, "You will become a Sakkaraya (cupid) man! Don't misuse it. Okay. Now go for a hot bath."

Vedamahaththaya was really happy.

Following day Vedamahaththaya summoned me and asked about the full story.

He treated me very well. When he learnt that I am a victim of insurgency. I thought he will get panicked. No He didn't. He said he has treated so many cases of these brave insurgents. But now he feels it is not so safe for me to be in this house. If army comes to know that I am with him it will have a bad reflection on him. Therefore he asked me to leave in disguise. He said as my beard is grown nobody could make me out now. He asked me to go to a faraway place and live quietly. He gave me some money. I knelt down and worshipped Vedamahaththaya, and thanked him and left his place.

"Tell me something about your personal life and how you were involved in this insurgency movement." DIG interrupted.

"Well Sir, I am from down South. From Karandeniya. There was a big estate next to our small property. My father was a "Bass", a carpenter. He approached the owner of the estate. He was a renowned criminal lawyer, one Silva from Colombo. My father used to work in his estate and lawyer likes him. He accompanied me to the lawyer.

He was fully satisfied with my education. I had passed my G.C.E. Advanced- level with full marks. My father said I am very clever but he has no money to give me a further education.

Can't possibly send to an university although I have passed the university entrance exam. Then the lawyer agreed to help me. He accompanied me to the Russian Embassy. After a discussion with the Ambassador I got the opportunity to go to Russia for further education. I thought it was a blessing in disguise Sir. A poor fellow like me getting an opportunity to go to Russia for further education. I was admitted to the Lumumba University. There I met comrade Rohana Wijeweera. While we were studding we were involved in several liberal movements and studied about such movements happening all over the world. Rohana was obsessed with the idea to take over the government after a well organized revolution. He formed the JVP in 1965. It is a long story Sir."

"It doesn't matter if DIG is interested you may relate it later, but now tell me where this Vedamahathaya was living?" doctor was inquisitive.

"He was living in an interior village at Kadugannawa. I went over there immediately after amnesty was declared. But I couldn't find him. His house has been demolished and a housing scheme has come up. I inquired from a nearby boutique.

They said the Vedamahaththaya had been abducted by the insurgent movement of the JVP and thereafter the walauwa had been demolished and a housing scheme had come up. I couldn't find any information about him. I don't know whether he is living or not. Now it is nearly 23 years. He was pretty old at that time. I believe that he is no more."

"Why don't you make a few attempts to find some information about him?"

It was DIG who put that question to his head assuming doctor would be interested to familiarize the technique and ingredients went into the whole process. He further said "We will give you every support from my end. I'll see what assistance that I could give."

He agreed.

"Then tell me something about you and your wife's child birth. Shall we summon her also?" DIG asked.

"If necessary Sir, but after I left physician's house I went in search of my home. However with a suspicion I went to my village. My house was no more there. Whole village has been destroyed, probably by the army. I went to Matara in search of some of my friends. I didn't meet any one of them. To my surprise, there I met a woman who was with me at Deniyaya transmitting station which we took over after killing the engineers who were there during the early uprising in 1971. There were two girls with me I had no sexual connection with either of them. We were not interested as our focus was on another direction. When we tried to operate the transmitter we saw army vehicles coming towards the station, we blasted the transmitting tower and ran away. They were shooting with rifles, one girl who was with me got a shot. Instantly she died. I carried the body and I asked the other one who was with me to run in another direction.

Somehow or other I escaped. The other one I referred Sir is my present wife. After the declaration of Amnesty she had unofficially married to a man.

When I met her she was so happy and she took me to her house and introduced to home people. Her husband has died and she has no children. She agreed to marry me. I was not in a position to do heavy work as four of my fingers in the left hand were chopped off. However I managed to do menial jobs and earned something. It was during this time my wife got pregnant. She didn't want to visit the hospital for check up. On the day she got labor pains she was admitted to Matara hospital. It was an impoverish hospital and there was only two doctors. Her pain was unbearable. It sustained for over a week. They got down a senior doctor from Colombo. With a surgery, he was able to deliver the child. It was a baby boy just more than six pounds in weight. Anyway doctor said it was a great battle and it was very lucky that mother escaped from death… It was an unusual birth. Doctors were astonished. Doctor said if she gets pregnant again she will die. So with my permission he performed an operation to remove the womb. With the child she had to be on the ground due to lack of beds. We had to face a bad time again.

Some of our former friends and enemies when they had come to know that I have returned and got married to this woman attacked her house and killed her mother and sister who were living there. They demolished the house.

I left the hospital with the wife and the child, but had nowhere to go. Incumbent doctor who noticed our difficulties suggested to us to give the child to someone who has no children to adopt. She was a Muslim lady. We gave over the child to her reluctantly.

Thereafter I met a fellow insurgent who is now working in a farm in Nuwara Eliya. He was the person who gave me the information about our enemy who killed my wife's mother and sister and demolished the house. I had taken that fellow's mother and the whole family during our insurgency period and kept in captivity. My friend asked me not to remain in Matara but invited us to go with him. We came over to Nuwara Eliya. It is a pity to tell Sir, by trying to help me he got into a big trouble. We had no money to live so he robbed money from the owner by killing him. Been an insurgent killer instinct had not diminished. He was caught by the police. I fled with my wife and survived in several places. Ultimately came across a farmer off Nuwara Eliya. He agreed me to help him. He built a mud hut for us and there we were living"

"Suraweera I am very particular about the wonder drug

which the physician administered to you. Isn't there anywhere else you can find out the prescription?"

I have my doubts Sir. I have never heard from any quarter a remedy like this. Native physicians when they die their system also have a natural death. They never ever teach secret medicinal recipes to anybody else. If there is a reliable pupil of course likely to be considered. Otherwise with their death everything will disappear."

"What a pity!" Doctor lamented.

"This is the prevailing system here with old physicians, Doctor. They never give out secrets. With their deaths everything will die and disappear." D.I.G. lamented.

"Suraweera you are a learned person. Your education now serves no purpose. Why don't you get the help from our minister's wife and get a job somewhere. With your education surely you can do something." D.I.G. proposed.

"Yes, Sir, But now I am psychologically expired. I have forgotten what I learned. Till I die I'll manage somehow or other. If I can stay here with my wife I am more than happy."

"Madam will definitely help. She is a philanthropist. Always ready to help any person in need. Well I feel sleepy now. If doctor wanted to know more about the childbirth you can ask your wife also to come here and describe everything to him. I'll go to sleep." He went out and tap at Dorothy's room. She opened the door. Were you listening into what we were talking?"

"Yes Donald. I feel very sorry about the fellow. I'll allow them to work here and give a suitable salary and look into their well being."

"Okay. Then you sleep. What time should we get up?"

"Anytime you like we can leave after lunch. I don't think Doctor is in a hurry to go."

"Let him discuss! Let's sleep."

Doctor summoned Suraweera's wife and had a long discussion with regard to her child birth.

"My child must be a sturdy boy now where ever he is living Doctor. He should be a grown up youth."

"I am sure if he had the opportunity to learn, as he is having my genes, I surmise he may have learnt well. I am always thinking about him."

"Now it is late at night you all go and sleep. We are leaving tomorrow."

"Don't have any fear now as you guys are with our good lady."

"Fear! He still gets frightened at night when he constantly dreams about the torture that he had suffered." Suraweera's wife uttered.

"Let by gone be by gone, Suraweera. Good night to you guys" Doctor left to the room assigned to him. Suraweera and wife switched off the lights and retired to their room."

Following day after lunch they left Nuwara Eliya.

Doctor spent one more day in the Island and arrived in Toronto, Canada.

Chapter 3
Cricket Match – Dance Competition

―――――――――◇―――――――――

"Lee I have to go to the Orchard early today. Could you prepare three omelets, bacon, some vegetables and six slices of bread. Brown bread for the doctor and arrange the breakfast table without delay." Mrs. Guptha addressed the house maid Wong Lee from the bed room itself. Her husband Dr. Guptha who was already up was flipping the Saturday Star. He referred to a half page advertisement with photographs and graphic relevant to the forthcoming dance championship to be held next Saturday at the Sheraton Hotel near the Toronto Airport. He requested his wife to show that to her daughter, Sitha who is a prominent participant in the competition and scheduled to perform a cabaret item at the end of the competition.

Within half an hour Lee prepared the breakfast and sounded the gong. Mrs. Judy Guptha went along and sat as she had to leave early to her Orchard at Brampton where the apple picking session is supposed to start by 10 in the morning. Doctor also came right away, with the paper and showed the advertisement.

"I have my dance practices at 10. I too have to go right away."

Said Sitha, their daughter, while coming towards the table.

"Prior to that have a glance at this advertisement." Mom handed over the paper to her daughter, showing the advertisement.

"Wow! What a magnificent ad, giving full prominence to my cabaret item. I am sure daddy, this item will bring me a great honour."

"You should perform it well!" Mama gave an encouragement by glancing at it.

"It's a very crucial dance item mama. Admixture of Bharatha, Kathakali and Rumba. It was choreographed by Mam. Supernova, but lots of ideas were given by me."

"Incidentally, Sitha and mom." Doctor came out with a suggestion. " Minister's wife Dorothy Senanayake is very interested to visit Canada. She has been to so many countries but so far has not got an opportunity to visit here. Why don't we invite her so that she can watch Sitha's Championship Show and her creation of this cabaret item?"

"Not a bad idea. But will there be sufficient time for her to obtain visa, ticket etc." Mrs. Judy Guptha asked.

"O, she is a very influential woman, after all she is a minister's wife. She can obtain everything within a day."

"In that case you may have to e-mail a suitable letter to be forwarded to Canadian Embassy in order to obtain visa."

"That's no problem."

"I too like to visit Sri Lanka. It is a country with plenty of archaeological remains and has a history of more than 2500 years. Moreover I like to learn something about their Kandyan dancing. Which I heard is unique and peculiar to the country."

"For that purpose you may have to stay there for a few months."

"Let's discuss when Mrs. Senanayake arrives here." Doctor suggested.

Mrs.Guptha after breakfast left to the orchard. Sitha left for the dancing hall where she is having her rehearsals.

Guptha families' orchard is situated at Heart Lake Road, Brampton, a 1, 000 hectare plot. There is a posh cottage bungalow with a swimming pool and a nice garden with plenty of flowers during the summer. Few days more to end the summer but still there are full bloomed flowers. Their brewery is fairly large and they brew ciders, syrup etc. They have earned a good name for their products as a result demand is fairly high.

The mini-zoo in the orchard is housed with so many animals. There is a separate staff to look after them. Next to the zoo there are apartments for the work force, which comes to about 25. Most of the male workers are from Guyana and Trinidad. Females are all from Canada. Most of the males from Guyana and Trinidad come only when the work started.

Dr. Guptha and family live in a very tall condominium in Toronto, which has 75 stories. They are in a luxury unit, with ultra modern furniture's and amenities. Separate room for gym as all the three are particular about their health and physiques. A posh room has allocated even for the cook woman, Lee.

Mrs. Guptha is a pretty lady of proportionate features. She is a Canadian; of course her grandparents migrated from Britain. When she visited India she had met the doctor. She had an attack of Asian flu and admitted to the hospital in New Delhi. There she met the doctor who was an intern. They were fallen in love and got married in Canada. Sitha is their second child. First child died at delivery. Thereafter Doctor decided to follow gynecology with a great enthusiasm and dedication. He was involved in research to discover modern methods and techniques. In addition he developed several psychological approaches to reduce risk and pain of the mothers. His latest development on embryo therapy was his own creation and experimented several years to achieve prospective results. He was a Hindu by birth. But did not adhere to primitive observations and had meager faith on the pantheon. But had a profound love on the philosophy. He says in Hinduism there is only one God. That's the Brahaman. An Absolute. Just like the Sun. Sun has so many rays. Similarly Hindus have created a big pantheon with so many Gods and Goddesses, just like the rays of the Sun. They will create more and more Gods and Goddesses. Even from legend stories they create deities. Last they created, according to what he believes, God Hanumantha. A monkey God. It was from Ramayana.

During his younger days he attended Hindu Temples to perform pooja (offerings) but once he became a senior doctor he totally gave up attending Temples or observing any poojas. He was self reliance. Sitha was in between. She goes to church with the mother and once in a way attends Hindu temples. She learned Indian dancing from an exponent of Bhrarath and Kathakali, Mrs.Luxami Devanarayan.

She was a very devoted, cultured woman who had enormous faith on Hindu gods and goddesses. Because of her dance teacher Sitha was compelled to observe Saraswathi pooja regularly.

It was because of the same reason that she was interested in later stages to follow archeology. Indian archaeologists perform poojas prior to commence any archaeological excavation. In Canada of course, there are no such remains to be excavated. Canada has a very short history.

Dr. Guptha after e-mailing the letter pressed her number and extended the invitation requesting her to arrive on Saturday to witness Sitha's dance competition. Message was recorded in the voice mail.

Little while later she confirmed the trip over the phone. She said her travel agent arranged everything and informed flight will touch down at 6.00 am on Saturday at the Pearson Airport in Toronto. She will be accompanied by Minister's body guard, Faizal.

Doctor was so happy. Immediately he informed his wife to make itinerary and notify Sitha who was at the dancing theater. Further he revealed that she is being accompanied by the Minister's Body Guard, popular cricketer Faizal.

"Dada, then I must convey the message to Hellings who has arranged a match with the visiting West Indies team and he would be delighted to get Faizal into his team."

"Not a bad idea."

"First I'll get in touch with Hellings and if he desires, dada could give a call and request Mr.Faizal whether he is willing to play."

"I could do that, first you talk to Hellings and when you return home for lunch. I'll initiate a call."

"Okay Dada."

Meanwhile Mrs.Guptha phoned up and informed she could order lunch from Mandarin and asked doctor to advise Lee not to prepare lunch for them. She asked when Sitha returns to come with her.

Immediately Sitha returns home, Sitha said Hellings is very eager to get Faizal to his team and to contact him and find out whether he is willing to play. Doctor said now they must be sleeping. But, agreed to leave the message in the voice mail.

The following morning itself Faizal had given a ring.

"He has told that he has never played cricket in a foreign country, although he would be little tired due to the hectic journey and despite months out of the game he said he is willing to play."

Doctor summoned Sitha and conveyed the message. She immediately informed Hellings.

Hellings reconstructed the team in order to accommodate Faizal.

On the day of their arrival Hellings with the Organizer, Mr. Mendis went over to the Airport. At that time Dr. and Mrs.Guptha already had gone to the arrival and was waiting for their guests.

When Mrs. Senanayake and Vibhisana Faizal arrived, they were introduced to Mrs.Guptha and then to Hellings and Mendis.

Hellings said he wish to accompany Mr.Faizal straight to the stadium. But on the contrary doctor proposed to take them to the Hotel and allow them to get rest for half an hour.

They agreed and went straight to the Sheraton Hotel, adjacent to the Airport. Mrs. Senanayke said he must have a bath before the breakfast and Faizal also wanted to have a shave and a body -wash. Until they return Mendis and Hellings were waiting in the lobby.

When Faizal came over to the lobby, they went straight to the stadium. On the way they discussed their arrangements.

Match had been scheduled to start at 10.00 in the morning and Hellings introduced Faizal to the team who were eagerly waiting for his arrival at the Stadium.

Having taken breakfast Faizal proposed to have little practice as there is little more time to start the match. They all went to the ground and practice with their coach Leanage.

When they were practicing Lara and party also came out to have a short practice.

At ten o'clock, umpire had the toss which was won by Lara and decided to bat first as the pitch was placid.

Chandrapaul, their ace batsman started the opening batting. His very first shot was a magnificent sixer. Bowling was done by Joy. He tried to spin like Murali and got a wicket at the 3rd over. Wicket keeper was Suren. He was excellent! With a jump he caught the ball of Chandrapaul. Next was Lara. His scintillating strokes covered 20 boundaries. He had partnership with Samuel, John and Grait. He scored 215 and was out for a catch by Bimal. They played brilliant cricket and were all out for 420 by 1.15.

It was a huge target for the Canadian team consists of Hellings as the Captain, Mendis, their organizer, Suren the wicket keeper, Faizal and rest of the team, Bimal, Joy, Cheema, Cuga, Rohan, Jude, Nihal and Ranasinghe.

Faizal who played at the top order scored 250 with 30 boundaries and six towering sixes. Jude the left hand batsman with the glorious off side shots achieved 35.Hellings, a product of Maris Stella played with scintillating stroke almost similar to Sangakkara. The righthand batsman Ranasinghe got glorious 25 with five bounderies. Top middle and last orders played excellent cricket and Bimal was played the last stroke at the 50th over and wrapped with 420.Match became a draw. It was a brilliant mock match.

After the awarding ceremony all were opted to go to Hilton for dinner. But Faizal pleaded excuse as he has to be at the Sheraton Gate Way Hotel to watch the Championship dance competition of Dr. Guptha's daughter. Hellings gave a ride to Faizal to the hotel. Dr.Das Guptha was waiting for him.

National News Papers and Sri Lankan tabloids such as Reporter, Ceylon Express, Dasatha in Canada had given full publicity with pictures and lengthy write ups. One Sinhala paper, Yathra had given a bio-sketch of Faizal with one of his action pictures.

Guptha had to give few minutes to Faizal who said he must have a wash and a change. Meanwhile Guptha was chatting with Hellings until Faizal returns. Hellings thanks profusely to Faizal and requested him to make another trip to Canada.

The Sheraton banquet hall was decorated beautifully and either side had been fixed with very broad rain curtains. When multi-color flash lights focus on them they were gleaming magnificently. That added an unbelievable back ground to the dancers and the dance floor.

The opening dance item was a Latin American Tango where exactly ten young couples took the dance floor amidst a thundering applause. Sitha danced with a black boy. He was the partner for her Championship competition. Next item was a Samba and Cha Cha which heightened the enthusiasm of the audience. They moved with incredible speed through intricate footwork and pirouetting, spinning, insisting bit of a jive of the band.

After a short break Championship competition started very gracefully where all the ten couples participated. Sitha's jewelries and the sophisticated costume were equally magnificent. Her partner was wearing a black tuxedo with a red waist band and a red bow. They danced to the scintillating rhythms of the Orchestra. Sitha had actually an amazing acrobatic performance where her partner accompanied gave full support to enhance her movements. Both of them were very cleverly twisting, gliding and were swift like lightening.

It was an unequivocal performance recently people watched in a dance floor. At the end there was a continued applause for about two minutes. It took nearly another two minutes for the judges to announce the results. It was no other than Sitha Guptha and Brian Pollocks adjudged as the winners. After awarding the trophy organizers announced that a special cabaret item will be performed by the winning candidate, Sitha Guptha as illustrated in the agenda. Until she changed her costume Leader of the Niagara Orchestra will be presenting Beethoven 9th symphony. "Let's appreciate" said the presenter. Amidst the applause Mr.Fiddale Jurgan started conducting the orchestra.

It didn't take more than five minutes for Sitha to have a change. Immediately after the performance of the Orchestra was over she gracefully appeared on the floor. Her cabaret composed of Bharatha natyam, Kathak, Ramba and Samba. Indian, drummers, Dholak and Murdangam accompanied in addition to the western orchestra. Dance is one way of communication. With this item she attempted to convey the value of unity of mankind.

She started with Namaste dance of Bharath natyam which was completely different set of movements from the any of the western modalities. At the start it was a slow movement but gradually accentuate with fast dramatic movements.

Then again slowed down with graceful movements of Kathak and swiftly changed in to Samaba and Rumba. With a graceful body movement she went back to Bharath and wound up with a Namaste. The audience gave her a thundering applause.

Once the performances were over they had dinner at the Sheraton and went home around 1.00 am.

Following day was a Sunday. Dr. Guptha had been summoned by the Hospital for a complicated childbirth of a sixty six year old Indian woman who delivered triplets. Mrs. Guptha, Sitha and Faizal with Mrs. Senanayake went to the orchard after their breakfast at the apartment. On the way they discussed about Sitha's Championship competition and Faizal's cricket, which were appeared prominently in several news papers.

National News Papers and Sri Lanka tabloids in Canada had given full publicity with pictures and lengthy write ups on the cricket match. Along with cricket news, Sitha's Championship pictures also had been published in Canadian News Papers, such as The National, The Sun, The Toronto Star and Globe and Mail.

Immediately they arrived at the Bungalow at the orchard Mrs. Guptha asked Sitha to order lunch from Mandarin.
"Isn't it too early mom?"
"Never mind! Let them deliver around 12.30."

She placed an order for Chinese for five in anticipating dad also to call over.

Mrs. Senanayake desired to go on a shopping spree with Mrs.Guptha. Mrs.Guptha said she will go on a round of supervision and agreed to accompany her. She also wishes to go with her if it won't be an hindrance.
"No, no come let's go" Both of them first visit the boutique and then the brewery and returned in thirty minutes. Thereafter both of them hopped in to the car and left.

Faizal and Sitha stayed back as Faizal said he is willing to go on apple picking although he was in Germany he didn't get an opportunity to visit an orchard. They moved and along with other visitors got in to a truck and proceeded to the one end of the orchard and got down along with the rest.

"This orchard was purchased by my dada only two years back for a fortune. He is a person who liked Ramayana very much. So he re-registered this as Dasaratha.'

"That must be the reason why you were christened as Sitha?"

"Probably. Dasaratha was the King, that was Rama's father."

"Although he is busy with medicine and medical research and various other research activities, he purchased a winery in Niagara Region, which also registered as Dasaratha as he is so fond of Ramayana. We are visiting there tomorrow. Have you seeing Niagara Falls?"

"Only in pictures" He picked up an apple from a branch and asked Sitha, "What do you called this variety? It is very sweet."

"You like sweet? There are several sweet varieties. This is known as Red Delicious. Try a few more verities and select your favorites."

"My policy is to taste all the varieties."

"Oh, it is impossible. We have about 100 varieties here. All over the world there are more than 6000 varieties according to recent research conducted by experts."

"You have sufficient time to take an interest on apple growing?'

"For anything I could find time. As dada is taking an enormous interest, along with his busy schedule, I had to lend my hand."

"So, tell me something about apple growing" While munching an apple Faizal asked.

"Well, in Spring tiny leaves begin to unfold in every twigs of apple trees where there are sufficient water, light and air for the trees. Then spring flowers. When the petal fall off fruits are bearing. I don't think you need the entire process."

"No, no. It will take a long time."

While picking some more apples, he asked, "Can I select each from every variety for me to take home?"

"Absolutely no objection! If the weight won't become an hindrance."

"Oh, I can carry any weight."

"No I mean in the flight."

"No problem! So long as madam Senanayake is there problem won't crop up."

"Commercial quantity will not be allowed at your Customs?"

"No problem. Our Custom does not check our madam. We have the right to use the VIP gate."

So saying he picked different verities and dump them in polythene bags, while munching bit by bit in other varieties and throwing the rest.

He collected different varieties into two other bags and suggests, "Now shall we go back. I wanted to have a shower."

"Then let's go. Give me one bag. I'll carry."

" Don't insult me. I have the potency to carry even more."

"Yeah! When look at your body, anybody can assume."

Faizal had an excellent physique with sturdy hands and a deep cleft in the chin.

They passed the crowd and returned to the bungalow. "Before we get our lunch I like to have a shower bath. Then we can have a hot lunch."

"Why you don't want to wait till mom comes?"

"When women go shopping you never know what time they will return."

"I agree."

" Well there are two wash rooms. There is a Shower in one. The other has a tub."

"I prefer the shower."

She accompanied and said there are different kinds of shampoos. You may use whatever you prefer."

"Thank you." he entered but didn't latch the door.

Little later while having the shower he noticed there was no bath towel, so he called Sitha, "I am sorry, I couldn't ask for a towel."

"O, isn't there a towel? I'll bring in a moment."

She came with a towel and as the door was opened she stretched the hand saying "Here's the towel Faizal. Oh my god!" she tried to escape but Faizal pulled and gave her a bone cracking hug and an alluring kiss on her temple. She tries to escape. But Faizal pressed his lips on her cheek. Instinctively her lips opened and he merged his lips gently. It was unexpected and explosive. She heard a sound of a vehicle, "Lunch may have arrived, I'll go." She slipped.

Yes the Mandarin car was at the door step. The Boy pulled out two boxes. "Where am I to keep?"

"Take straight to the dining room. He kept that and brought another two boxes and handed over the receipt gadget. Sitha signed on it as they have an account at Mandarin. Before he left arrived Mrs. Senanayake and Mom. She asked "Why so early?"

"Big crowd child. Couldn't possibly select anything. So we returned."

"It is good. Then we can have hot lunch." Sitha turned to mom and said "Dada is not coming mom. He said he will have some snack from the cafeteria of the hospital. He is having a patient in critical condition. So he had to stay back."

"Then let's go and arrange the table." She went in with Sitha.

After the bath Faizal also came out.

Mrs. Senanayake with an exhausted look sat on a chair.

"After lunch I must have a nap."

"Yes aunty, you can do that. I'll arrange lunch with mom."

"You didn't buy anything?" Faizal asked. .

"Only a few things. Not worth wasting time. So we returned."

Mrs.Guptha came and invited Dorothy and Faizal to have lunch.

After the lunch Dorothy went for a wash and retired for a nap. Mrs.Guptha accompanied her to the room.

Sitha cleared the table with the help of Faizal and they came to the patio. Flowers had bloomed beautifully in few of the plants others have faded already. Faizal admired very much of the remaining flowers and greeneries. He sat on a garden chair along with Sitha, "You do the gardening too?"

"I do sometimes along with dada and mama, but there are boys in the orchard who attend to all these work. So, so now tell me something about you Faizal." Sitha requested earnestly.

"Well, I am a sub-inspector attached to Sri Lanka police force. I Joined two years back after obtaining BA in Peradeniya University. I had my training at the Police Academy at Katukurunda and in the Police training School in Cologne. I served at the Police Head Quarters for some times and affiliated to a DIG in a sub division. Presently I serve as a Body Guard to Minister of Religious Affairs. I play as a free lancer of the National Cricket Team."

"How is your married life?"

"Fortunately I am not yet chained."

"There can't have any restriction in Sri Lanka Police for a person to get married. How is your girl friend?"

"I don't have a particular girl friend as such. But there is one girl who is very close to me…"

"…and she is going to be your future married partner?" She completed an inadequacy.

"May be or may not be. She was my batch mate at the University, Kumari Amunugama. We were at the same Hall. Mars Hall. We joined the Police force together. Had training together at the Police training Academy. Had the advanced training in Cologne and Munich in Germany together."

"That suggests you may also have flirted together!" She had a hearty laugh.

"I won't say no. In our University almost all the boys had girl friends. At least for 75%. They all flirt. Nothing to hide. Near the University there is a jungle plot, called Hanthane. So all the couples go there and flirt. It is a well known secret."

"Well known secret! Any interesting incident?"

"There are. I highlight one. That is the day she lost her virginity…"

"Ah!"

"In that jungle we went little further away from other couples and we enjoyed thoroughly. She said bit painful. I just looked at her skirt. There was lot of blood. I raised the skirt, in both thighs there were several leeches. One has got crushed and blood oozed all over. I didn't want to pull them out rashly. It is bad. Somehow or other I slowly removed one by one. Wiped all the blood. I pulled out my shirt and asked her to wrap around. We avoid the crowd and crept through another foot path and went to a dispensary. Apothecary cleared everything and used some medications and bandaged. This incident I'll never forget."

"That's a daring experience!"

"Absolutely!"

"So, she doesn't press you to get married?"

"No Sitha, so far she has not made any such suggestion. Why should I be impatient?"

"And you are in love with her?"

"No such binding. I don't hate any one and that suggests I love everyone." He said amusedly.

"You are very frank." Then her cell rang. She took out the cell "Yes, yeah dada, Mrs. Senanayake is sleeping and mom went on a supervision round, there she comes. Mom dada."… She gave the cell to mama.

The Doctor said his duties are over and asked whether to go home or to call over there. She asked him to come over to the orchard and wound up the conversation.

"Dad is coming over here. Where shall we go?"

"We can go for a movie or to watch a game of ice hockey or basket ball …"

"Madam won't be interested." Faizal responded.

"I thought as much perhaps a movie she may like" Mrs. Guptha suggested.

"Although this is a vast country, there aren't much things to see." Sitha quips.

"In that respect in our little island there are plenty of things to see."

"Yes Faizal. We discussed with dada also for me to go over to Sri Lanka for my PhD after obtaining MA here. I sat for it. The Results are likely to be out today or tomorrow."

"Ideal! We can provide all your requirements."

"Yeah, that should be discussed with Mrs. Senanayake, perhaps to night." Mrs. Guptha commented.

They were chatting in the patio till Dr. Guptha comes. When he arrived they got up and went inside, by the time Mrs. Senanayake was up.

Someone suggested to go for a movie as there was nothing outstanding event or a place to visit.

They went to Cineplex where there are eight cinema halls and eight movies are screened.

After arriving at the Hall only they decided what to watch.

"There is Dr.No. It is a thrilling spy movie, but fairly old." Dr. Guptha suggested.

"Although it is old Mrs. Senanayake may like it." It was from Faizal.

"If I won't feel sleepy, I don't mind."

"It is interesting Dorothy, you may not feel sleepy. I saw it when I was in India."Mrs.Guptha said.

"Then it must be pretty old."

"Fairly, I watched it when I was attending college."Faizal said.

Anyway they decide to buy tickets and Mrs.Guptha went to the counter.

"It is the first movie of James Bond, written by Ian Fleming. He wrote this when he was in Jamaica. Even the movie was shot in Jamaica. James Bond was portrayed by Sean Connery. Brilliant actor" Dr. Guptha elaborated.

"I think he had several James Bond Movies. But I am not much interested for just thrills. Because there are no substances, a reality." That was Sitha's idea.

"Yes, Ian Fleming had written several, such as Russia with love, Gold finger, Thundeball. After the death of Ian several other writers continued the series. There, mom has bought the tickets. Let's go."

Dr. Guptha suggests when Mrs.Guptha was coming towards them with tickets.

They entered the Hall. There were not much of a crowd. May be because movie is fairly old. It was produced in 1963. Younger generation today like latest movies with modern technological gimmicks with computer manipulations. However the party seemed to be quite complaisant with the movie.

"Where shall we go for dinner?" Dr. Gupta asked when they were coming out of the complex.

"As we had a Chinese lunch, shall we go for an Indian dinner." Sitha suggested.

"You guys had Chinese but I had only a snack. Dorothy may like Indian."

"If Dorothy likes, we don't mind."

"They use too much spice. But for a change I don't mind.

They went for an Indian restaurant in Toronto and enjoyed the food thoroughly.

When they returned to the Condominium their discussion was on Sitha's trip to Sri Lanka "You come darling, we have fairly a big house. You can stay with us. I don't have children. I'll look after you as one of my own. You can attend Peradeniya University. There are so many archaeological sites in Sri Lanka. I'll take you to all the places. You can obtain the highest academic qualification on archaeology at the Peradeniya University. It is a very famous place."

"No doubt, Dorothy will provide all your requirements. But we will send you enough money." Dr. Guptha suggested.

"Money is no problem. I have enough money. You make arrangement to go with us.

We will accompany you.

"In that case I am very eager to visit Ajantha and Khajuraho on our way."

Faizal intervened. "In that case we have to change our itinerary. It is simple, we can inform our Agent. He will arrange everything."

"Attend to it Faizal. Before leaving to Niagara you may arrange everything in the morning." Mrs. Senanayake proposed.

"I'll give a ring now itself. Now it is early morning in Sri Lanka. The Agent has enough time to make arrangements."

"Go ahead."

"How about Sitha's visa?"Mrs.Guptha asked.

" We can obtain it. No problem." quips Dr. Guptha.

"All of us need visas to India too."

"That's simple tomorrow morning we can arrange before you all are leaving to Hellings.

Why not we initiate a call to Hellings now?" Dr. Guptha pulled out the cell from his pants.

"Hellings, Dr. Guptha here, Your friends will drop in to your place for tea tomorrow morning on their way to Niagara..."

He had asked them to come for lunch on returning from Niagara. Then Faizal came over and Doctor handed over cell to Faizal. He has told him that they will come over to his place for breakfast. Hellings had told that they can come for breakfast also, but very eager to see them at lunch. Faizal inquired others and they agreed to go over there for lunch, Faizal confirmed Helling's request.

Following day after attending to all their requirements including visas, they left to Niagara around 10.30 in the morning.

CHAPTER 4
Visit to Niagara Falls

———————◇———————

"Niagara may be the largest water fall in the world." Mrs. Senanayke opened up a chat on the way to their destination.

"No aunty." While driving Sitha remarked. "Largest is the Victoria Falls in Africa. It is about one mile long. But Niagara is the most picturesque. It has two falls. American Falls and Canadian Falls. The Canadian Falls you have to look from up. In 1931 this was totally frozen."

"If you provide all the details in advance the thrill will be lost."

"Absolutely!"

"You must stay one night in a hotel here and watch the grandeur." Mrs.Guptha suggests.

"Time is the problem." Mrs. Senanayake said.

"What are the good hotels at Niagara?"

"There are so many Faizal. Couple of months back we came to Niagara and stayed overnight at Great Wolf Lodge. That was a village type interior hotel with a massive water park. I enjoyed a lot but not mama and dada."

"That was good for children." Mrs.Guptha quips.

"They were more interested to stay closer to our winery."

"We must visit the winery." Dorothy suggests.

"Yes aunty on our way."

They switch on to discuss on the Winery. "It is at the Niagara on the lake. That is in the Niagara region. The best area thawing grapes for ice wine.

When we engage on the tour our experts will demonstrate all the details and aunty can purchase a few bottles after tasting."

"I must, I must."

"You may like ice wine. It is the best. Ice wine made out of frozen grapes."

"That's right. Dr. Guptha when he came to our place he had brought three bottles. They were sweet and very nice. I will buy about a dozen."

"O aunty, can you take so much?"

"Aunty will have no problem." Faizal commented.

When they arrived at Niagara, they parked the vehicle at the car park and tread down to watch the Horse Shoe Falls. There was a massive crowd. But that was no problem. They leaned against the parapet wall and kept on watching the beauty of the tumbling down of the fall from the elevated place. Mrs. Senanayake used her camera and snapped from several angles.

"If you are willing to have a thrilling view from the below, there is an elevator goes down to 150 feet where there is an observation deck or could sail by the boat, Maid of the Mist."

"let's go down." Faial was very eager. All of them bought tickets and they were given rain coats free of charge and they went down by the elevator. In a minute they arrived at the platform.

"It's slippery!" Dorothy remarked.

"Don't go to the edge aunty." Sitha was holding her hand.

"I like to go by the boat also." Faizal suggests.

They returned and by Niagara shuttle bus proceeded to the Maid of the Mist where they were provided with rain coats again to cover from top to bottom. It was an ace-thrilling trip where they sailed up to the bottom of the fall and it was amazing to look up with the thundering roar. To cover the entire trip you must get the excitement of soaring above the turbulent rapids and cascading waterfalls from the sky by riding in a helicopter.

Helicopter- ride is unique and spectacular experience. Helicopter service available from 9 am till sun set. Although there were so much of things to watch time didn't permit so they went straight to the Dasaratha Winery where they were welcomed by the senior staff. As they were willing to go for a tour Sitha accompanied them after tasting different samples of wines. At the lobby, Mrs.Guptha opted to stay behind as she was eager to look into accounts and other administrative matters. Group went to the vineyard and after demonstration went down the underground sparkling wine cellar. Although Mrs. Dorothy is a wine lover she was bit exhausted but enjoyed the trip.

One full case of different variety of wines kept inside the vehicle on the order of Mrs.Guptha. After returning from the demonstrative trip Faizal proposed to leave as Hellings must be waiting for them. Incidentally their orchard as well as winery were christened with the same name as Doctor has high regard for Ramayana.

Sitha drove pretty fast and within 45 minutes. they were in Hamilton. Hellings who was at the entrance of the basement as they have already sold their pub upstairs.

Faizal introduced others to Hellings and he introduced his beloved wife, Susila. They entered in and seated comfortably.

"How long you have been abroad?" Faizal asked.

"Well, it is a long story. I left Ceylon two rupees in my hand. I was in Germany. A Father helped me a lot. I got into a chain of hotels, Kolping House, as a cook and became specialized in Sri Lankan menus and was appointed as the Chef. From there I went back to Sri Lanka, got married to my beloved wife. I met her at Madu prior to my migration, at that time she was a minor. After marriage came to Canada. Now nearly 37 years. So I have decided to go back to my mother country, Sri Lanka."

"Oh, you are leaving Canada."

"I have sold my house. My business- bar upstairs, I have already sold. I bought a house for my son and daughter. They prefer to stay in Canada. The house is being refurbished. Once that is over we are shifting from here, and sell this too. Already bought a house and property in Sri Lanka."

"Where in Sri Lanka?"

"In my home town where I was born and bred. Negambo."

"Negambo! Where about?"

"It is at the Temple Road."

"We are also in Temple Road."Mrs. Senanayake responded.

"Pleasure to hear that! Give me a minute. I'll bring something to drink."

He brought the trolley with several bottles of liquor.

"We will have something very light. Sitha has to drive." Mrs.Guptha proposed.

"Sitha you like a soft drink."

"Yes Susila."

"I too prefer a soft drink."Mrs. Senanayake said.

"No you can have a glass of Champagne." He opened up the bottle and pour to glasses.

"Sitha too can have Champagne, it is not strong."

"No, better to have a soft drink. Here the police is very strict. You can't drive after liquor." Mrs.Guptha concluded.

Susila brought two glasses of mango drinks.

However Mrs. Senanayake too had Champagne.

"You find mango here?" Mrs. Senanayake inquired.

"In Canada you find anything." Hellings responded while pouring Red Label to a glass for Faizal.

"Whisky during this time is too strong."

"Red Label is not that strong."

"We have brought you a bottle of Red Wine from our winery." Mrs.Guptha said.

"Thank you so much Mrs.Guptha."

They had a pleasant conversation and Susila informed that lunch is ready.

"Yeah, let's have lunch soon. We have to make our itinerary as we are leaving tomorrow." Faizal got up with the glass in hand.

"Take your own time." Hellings proposed.

After lunch they left the place and arrived in one hour's time at Guptha's Condo.

"As dada is here shell we discuss little more about my trip to Sri Lanka?"

Sitha proposed.

"What is there more to discuss child, I'll look after everything. There is absolutely no problem for you."

"No aunty, I know that I'll have no problem. As we are visiting Ajantha and Khajuraho, I may like to have some information prior to visit the places."

"That of course your look out. But I don't think it is really necessary. They have their information centers. Once we go there we could collect all the informative bulletins you required." Faizal commented.

"Yes child that won't be a problem." Doctor said. "Even now if you scan the Internet you would be able to collect all what you need."

"Yes Dada, I'll go to the computer."

After she went to the room, Doctor said "Ajantha is a place where there are nearly 29 cave temples with Buddhist and Jaina frescos and sculptures. Whereas Khajuraho is a place full of erotic sculptures. It is a massive place, Entire village is the museum. Earlier there were 80 Hindu temples but now there are only a few. I have visited the place." Doctor explained.

"Sitha could learn all what is interested to her once she goes there." It was from Faizal.

"Judy now it is almost seven. Now let us think about a place where we could have dinner."

"Let's go to Hilton."

"I prefer to have something typical Canadian."

"We don't have any such places as Canadian. Canada is a pot puri of cultures. In that case we like to take you all to an exquisite place, CN Tower restaurant. From there you can have a scenic view of the entire Toronto. Very beautiful!"

"There is a rotating restaurant."

"Yes Faizal. It is1820 ft.high. At night entire Toronto could be seen. It is like heaven.

"In Religious domains illustrate heavens as places where everything is available. So these First World countries, could be treated as heavens to the people in the Third World countries." Mrs. Senanayake surmised.

"Perhaps!" Dr. Guptha was not quite sure.

They got ready, as it is somewhat customary, in First World countries to dress well when they go for dinner although the event is not so functional.

They climbed up by the elevator and entered in to the rotating area and sat on a table in the revolving section.

"This is like heaven!" Faizal uttered while looking outside.

"For us, the first world is just like heaven." Mrs. Senanayake said and look beneath. "As you said it is like heaven, so much of lights."

"When we look up on a clear day night, you can see millions of stars, you believe it is to be heaven. Stars are gods to highly religious minded people. When they think about god, they always look up. They feel and think god is up. So the sky above is heaven for them."

Doctor annunciates, "But here when you look down you see the glittering lights. So you can't call it heaven."

"Neither Hell!" Faizal quips. Meanwhile Sitha looks into menu charts and place the order in consultation with others. As all of them, except doctor had a heavy lunch, they ordered soup and a variety of dishes with lots of vegetables.

They were chatting lot about the luxury in Canada and were repenting that they could not stay for few more days.

After the dinner they returned home and discuss further on Sitha's University education.

They got a call from the travel Agency in Sri Lanka and Faizal attended to it.

Sri Lankan Travel Agency says arrangements could be made to visit Ajantha and Khajuraho from New Delhi or Mumbai. But they advised either to visit Ajantha and Ellora in Aurangbad which are closer from Mumbai or Khajuraho from Delhi. It will take a lot of time to cover all the three places. In Khajuraho you find sadistic sculptures which you don't find anywhere else in the world. Sculptures are mostly based on Vathsyayana's Kama Sutra. Worthwhile visiting! It is in the Maddhya Pradesh about 620 kilometers from East of Delhi. Can take a domestic flight. The Agency needs immediate response to make necessary arrangement."

"I prefer Khajuraho. Other places Sitha can visit later" Dorothy proposed.

"That's Okay aunty. Let's ask them to make necessary arrangement including hotel accommodation, if necessary."

Sitha agreed.

Faizal immediately telephoned and notified their requirements.

"So then that's Okay."

Following day they boarded an Air Canada flight and flew to New Delhi. They were there in the early morning.

From there they were taken to Khajuraho by a domestic flight of Air India. By a taxi they visited the Khajuraho and were amazed by seen erotic sculptures.

"Aren't these obscene aunty?" Sitha amazed.

"Well child, these may have carved several centuries back with colossal amount of money and time, not just for the fun. There must have a deep significant. Among human beings sex is a prime requirement for healthy and mutual living. When they are ignorant of this science their family life will be collapsed. That is my personal view.

But the creators of these sculptures must have had deep conceptions. Well, well, well, some are of course seemed obscene." Dorothy deliberated.

"There are brochures. With which you can get a broad idea." Faizal commented.

After spending nearly one hour they proceeded to the Taj Hotel which had been prearranged by the Travel Agency.

When they were returning by Sri Lankan Airline they were in the centre three seats and engaged in conversation further from brochures what they observed. This generated a romantic relationship between Sitha and Faizal. It was after the dinner and chief steward off the main lights to enable passengers to sleep. Dim lights highlighted the romantic atmosphere for Sitha and Faizal.

"Is madam asleep?"

"faster."

"I feel like giving you a kiss."

She was eagerly waiting for a moment "Are you paralyzed?"

"O, no! He hugged her, his lips got closer to her dainty lips, instinctively her lips parted.

She felt the warmth of his breath on her face. He gave a lingering kiss. Both of them wrapped with the blanket and was cuddling each other. They had a sparkling time until they reach the Katunayake Airport.

When they returned home there was an urgent message from DIG. Gampaha, in the voice mail.

"Madam, I have to go this evening to raid a brothel house. I am too tired and prefer to have a nap now."

"No objection!"

In the evening, around five, he left to D.I.G.'s office at Gampaha.

" I was wondering why you are late!"

"We arrived only in the morning, Sir." It was a tiring journey. Any way I am ready to take your assignment."

DIG briefed him everything and provided a team comprised with police cop to drive the van as well and three other woman police officers along with S.I. Amunugama.

Faizal clad with a saggy jacket and went over there as a decoy by a car. By that time his supporting team had been parked about twenty yards away from the spot near a bend. A middle aged woman was seated at the foyer and was reading a news paper.

"Good evening madam!"

"Good evening! What can I do for you? Have a seat."

"Don't bother I don't have much time. I have to take the

train to go to Kandy. I thought I could spend about one hour. That's why I came. What are your rates?"

"Well there are two categories. Those who are up, 450/- down 250/-"

"I prefer 250/-"

"Jane," She summoned a maid. Take this gentleman to corner room. You may go with her. Before that, pay me 250/- bucks"

He immediately paid the money and the maid accompanied him. She pointed out the room.

She tapped at the door."

I thought you are the person selected for me?"

"Oh! No." She disappeared. Faizal tapped at the door and it was opened by a well clad woman. Faizal introduced him as Ratnayake and seated on the bed.

"What's your name? Sit sit sit." She seated beside Faizal.

"What's your age?"

"I am twent… y… five"

"Are you married?"

"Yes."

"Any children?"

"I have two."

"What made you to select this job?"

"I have to feed my children and my mother. I couldn't get any other job."

"I feel sorry about you. How can I enjoy with a mother of two. I'll ask for somebody else."

"No no Sir, don't go."

He came out I need somebody else, a younger one. Then the police team entered.

Madam got bewildered. "You can go. You can go."

"Then give my money back."

"Here is your money. Go away, Go away." She went in.

By that time SI Kumari Amunugama with others arrested

all the women who were there including the house maid and came out. SI asked Faizal pretending he is not known to her, "What are you doing here?"

"I came to see the madam."

She hushed. "Then come with her." and they left to the van.

She came out covering her face.

"Madam you don't want to go with them?"

She didn't utter a word. She took her cell and hushed to someone. "Don't produce them to the court. I'll look after you.

They can't raid without a warrant!"

"I have the warrant." Faizal showed the warrant.

"Come I'll give you a lift."

He holds her hand and also showed his identity.

She was taken by his car to the Gampaha police station and handed over.

He immediately reported to DIG that Inspector deserves an immediate transfer," and discussed further in a lower tone and left.

DIG thanked him.

Meanwhile Madam got the Minister to originate a call to Vice Chancellor of the Peradeniya University. Which he did, and talked about her requirements. To enroll Sitha Guptha and provide her with hostel facilities.

Vice Chancellor agreed to look into everything.

CHAPTER 5
Mysterious Island – Hockey on Ice

———————◇———————

IGP telephoned Dorothy and requested her to release Faizal for an urgent investigation. She agreed. Following day morning he visited IGP.

"I summoned you Faizal to entrust you with a very special task. It sounds as an international racket. It ought to be a contraband smuggling spot or they must be having some mysterious affairs. Manipulate by some Sri Lankan and Maldivian racketeers. Our helicopters have spotted a boat coming from the region two days back. They have detected a tiny Island in the Indian Ocean. It is in the Sri Lanka waters. They have focused the light. I am sure now they must be perturbed a bit."

"They should have avoided that." Faizal quips.

"No one has ordered them to do so. As they got a bit of suspicion they have done that.

But you can't put the blame on them." IGP said. "First they have to know what it is to report the matter. Any way from their information now we know there is an island. It would be the place where they engaged in this smuggling. It has been camouflaged in such a way no plane would be able to detect it easily. So we have to raid the place. Arrest who ever there. Prime important thing is to detect what it is, get round the culprits who engaged in this racket. You have to be carefully traced the place and arrest everyone involved." IGP further said the whole affair will be handled by DIG. Abeysooriya. You go and meet him he will brief you what steps to be taken, and what facilities that he has already provided."

Faizal agreed to get in touch with DIG Abesooriya and thanked IGP and left.

DIG Abesooriya briefed him. "Faizal, this is a tiny island supposed to have emerged after the Tsunami in 26thDecember 2004. It is somewhere in the longitude of 79.769 and latitude of 8.233 but keep that as a secret don't announce it. Then somebody might pick it up. I have already arranged a makeshift Police station at the Riviera Maya Resort at the Karaitive Island. It is off Portugal Bay. I'll stay at the Alankuda beach hotel in Kalpitiya.

Radio link is also installed at the makeshift Police Station at the Resort, as well as in Alankuda beach hotel. ASP Thirugnasundaram and myself will be at this place. I am fully in charge of this operation. Inspector, Ronald Perera and your friend SI Kumari Amunugama and six cops have been already posted with five boats and one speed boat. At last night they left by now they may have gone to the Police Station at Karaitive. There Thiru is coming. Now let us leave. There are nearly 150 km to Kalpitiya from here. On our way will discuss further. They left by a jeep. On the way DIG said Helicopter engaged in patrol duty in the region will provide us with more and more information time to time.

When they arrived at Kalpitiya, they got in touch with the police team at the makeshift Police Station. DIG informed

ASP(Assistant Superintendent of Police) Thirugnasundaram and SI Faizal will come over there by a boat in couple of hours' time. Be prepared with everything necessary. Faizal will let you know the strategy and the time to raid.

On the very day a team comprised with IP, two S.I.'s and six cops in five boats allocated to them with radio transmitters and other facilities were ready to launch the raid. Around 2.00 am they got a radio message from the helicopter that was on petrol duty, to say a boat has gone to the island and returning to the Sri Lankan shore towards Puttalam. They hurriedly started and drive fast according to the direction indicated. ASP Thiru was at the Police station. When they were about half a nautical mile, off all the lights and row them by oars. When they reached closer to the isle, through binoculars noticed two fellows are there but both are sleeping. Inspector, Faizal, Kumari and three other cops got on to the isle. It was camouflaged with some material green in color and there was a hut. They landed from one side and approached slowly, cupped the mouths of the two watchers and put them down. Then they wrapped their mouths with glue bands and cuffed their hands from behind. Both of them were taken to a boat and tied them up.

They slowly entered the hut. A boy who was at the radio cubicle shouted, "There are some people!" Immediately he was got round, wrapped the mouth with tape and taken to a boat.

They could not extract much information from him. Before his mouth wrapped with the tape he uttered that there is a door on the floor to go down next to the Radio room. When they questioned what did you find there. He said he has never gone down. But he knows there are some women.

With that information, SI Amunugama got into a shirt and skirt and went down, kept the tiny mike attached to her dress. So that others on the top can hear what they speak. She did not take any weapon.

At that time all were except one was awaken.

"Hi, you are up. Boss has come."

"O I see! who are you?

" Boss's close friend Anita." She got seated on a posh chair.

"Which boss?

"Second in command."

Then two others got up. She introduced herself as the Supervisor and her name is Kathy. She is the most senior and in charge of the place. She is here for the last five years along with five others, after coming over here she said she had not seen the sun, moon, or stars but was enjoying thoroughly. Kumari had a laugh. Then she introduced other two who were up as Sashi and Miki. One is from Thailand. Other one is from Japan. Arrived last week with another three. Others also one by one got up.

"Are you guys are happy here?"

"Extremely happy!" It was obvious from the nightys that they were wearing and their posh look. Whole place was fully furnished with top class furniture and other amenities. Place had a fragrance of jasmine mixed with mimosa.

"Kathy I don't want to waste much time with conversation we have to evacuate this place as early as possible. Police have smelled a rat. You all will be taken to a better place where you can see the sun moon and stars. Boss is waiting up. So wake up others and pack up everything and get ready soon."

"Have we got to take all our things? Are we coming over here again?"

"Very unlikely."

Faizal came down. "O, What a nice place. A mini palace! With a jasmine smell!"

"Meet your Chief Security Officer, Mr. Suffique and she is Kathy who is in charge here.?" Kumari introduced.

"Welcome Mr. Sauffiqe. Shell we have some champagne?"

"No time Kathy. Time is precious!" Kumari quips.

"Mr. Suffique may like to see Ravana's observatory room?" Kathy again proposed.

"As Anita says time is precious, we have to go up soon, better five by five." Faizal said.

Anita requested recent recruit five to give their names to Suffique.

They came over and gave their names. Then a cop in civil came down. Faizal addressed to him. "Kenneth you take this five up and send to the boat." They went up.

Next five came up. "They came over here about a month back." Kathy commented.

Faizal jotted down their names and gave the board file to Kumari. "I'll take them you attend to the rest." So Faizal came up with next five. Meanwhile earlier lot has gone to the boat. IP had directed a cop to take them to a boat. "There are five more. Kumari will bring them up. I'll accompany these five to the boat." Faizal went down to the boat with them as he wanted to see how are their positions. He was satisfied. He advised, "Let the other five who will be coming now go to another boat." He ordered so as they are seniors and likely to talk unwanted things. He went up again. Meanwhile Kumari came with seniors. They had plenty of luggage. "Where is the Boss?" Kathy questioned.

"He has already gone to a boat." Faizal replied.

They were taken by another cop who came up and instructed him to take them to another boat. So that they will generate no suspicion.

Faizal proposed to the Inspector. "Shell we go down and have a thorough search?" He agreed. and all the three went down. "This is like a luxury palace no? Although it is small there are big TV screen and DVD machines!" Inspector uttered.

"This is an extraordinary posh brothel. An exhibition room of Ravana's observatory is also seems to be here. Could this cave have any connection to Ravana I wonder! "Faizal bewildered.

"You never know." Kumari said.

They investigated all the places and made a sort of an inventory.

"Two rooms are locked up." Kumari said to the Inspector. They broke opened both rooms. There were contraband and drugs.

"These women have been brain-washed and used as prostitutes. They are not the criminals. We have to arrest the criminals. That is the most important task, Sir." Faizal proposed to the Inspector.

"Yeah, we have to do that. Let's go up" Inspector proposed and they came up. He instructed Faizal and Kumari to stay behind and be vigilant. "I'll go back to the station and take all the women to custody and send them to a safe place in Alankuda Hotel."

Meanwhile if any boat arrives signal and identify and talk to me over the link. I'll be at the makeshift police station."

Inspector left. When he left Faizal and Kumari took four revolvers and went down again and found two places to hide themselves and were waiting to see anybody will come. Meanwhile they further check. There were generators, Air conditioners fitted right round. All exhaust pipes were seems to be jutted out and directed to the surface. There were enough liquor and fresh eatables. They tasted some of the eatables. They were wonderfully tasty.

They got a radio message from a copter to say a boat is arriving. They did not want to come up and preferred to wait in the cave, hide and see who would be the culprits.

Boat arrived. Anchored. Two fellows with rifles in hand and another tuff guy got out of the boat and climbed up. They found their guards and radio operator are missing. Two fellows, one with a rifle and other one with a revolver came down started checking. They noticed rooms have been forced open. Faizal shot at the person who had a rifle, exactly to his hand. Rifle was fallen down. Other one took out the revolver. Kumari shot at him. Then they came out and took their weapons, but had a tuft fight. Somehow or other they were controlled and hand cuffed and tied to a post.

Came up, noticed a man with a rifle, both of them shot at him. He was fallen down. Informed the Inspector. As ASP Thiru is at the station, he came with two cops in a speed boat. The two at down the cave were taken up and with the dead body of the slain person inspector went off. He further informed all the 15 women have sent to DIG at Kalpitiya who will make arrangement to send them to safe places.

Faizal and Kumari stayed behind.

Towards the early morning they noticed two speed boats are coming towards the isle from the direction of North East of Maldives. They signaled them when they were closer range, but there were no response. When they were coming closer they shot at them with a powerful rifle. One boat got burst. Other one came closer. Faizal and Kumari went back into the cave and hid themselves. Two fellows with revolvers came down. They were searching every nook and corner. Faizal and Kumari jumped upon them and had a dare- devil fight. They controlled both of them and hand cuffed. Wrapped their mouths and brought them up. There was no one in their boats. So they took them to their boat and sped up to the make shift police station and handed over to the Inspector.

They were informed that necessary arrangement had been made to interrogate all those who were arrested and launch further investigations. Faizal and Kumari were advised to return.

Later they learnt the cave in the Island was Ravana's observatory which had been washed off several thousand years back. It was earlier a mountain cave. After washed off, it has been drifted only after the tsunami on the 26th of December 2004. This had been surfaced during the tsunami and some business people from Sri Lanka in liaison with a Business people in Maldives have converted it to a posh brothel where they bring rich tourists for high rates to enjoy as they wish. Still they have not arrested the main criminals.

Fazal's assignment was over Further investigation was left to the DIG and his staff.

When Faizal returned home and reveled that it was like Ravana's observatory and articulated all what had happened. Sitha was very eager to visit the cave. But Faizal revealed that it has been sealed and open only once the investigation is over.

"Now your prime responsibility is your University enrollment Sitha. If you are really interested to see places Ravana associated you can find out from Suraweera who is at our Nuwara Eliya bungalow.

There is Sitha Amman temple and Suraweera knows a place where Ravana wrote his books. Give a call to him and get details. Now let's go to the University. On the way we may discuss further." Madam was ready to accompany Sitha to the Peradeniya University.

"If you are not too tired you can come with us to go to Peradeniya."

"No problem. I can come." Faizal agreed.

They went through Minuangoda, Nittambuwa, Warakapola and Mavanella to the University. Vice Chancellor had made all the required arrangements as requested by the Minister. So Sitha stayed back. Sitha has to return home every Friday evening. Mrs. Senanayake entrusted that responsibility to Faizal.

He undertook it without any hesitation. Faizal and madam returned. On the way they got down at Ambepussa and went to the rest house.

Although it is bit too late, a short description on Sitha for readers would be useful. Earlier I mentioned Sitha is the second child of Guptha family. Sitha is extremely beautiful although she didn't want to enter for a beauty queen contest. She is trim enough to catch the eye of any man. She has a beautiful dimple in her right cheek. Her slim body is ideal for a dancer. She is extremely gorgeous. Completing both elementary and secondary education in Toronto, she graduated with honors Bachelor of Art degree in history and prehistory with particular reference to ancient history of India and that region. She obtained Master of Art from the McMaster University in Hamilton. She is brave, bold and resourceful. She is well conversant with some of the Indian dancing's and that of the western. She had several public shows in number of cities in Canada and had earned a reputation.

Following day Mrs. Senanayake said that he has to go to the estate with Ranbanda to pluck coconuts. Faizal had to accompany the Minister.

Mrs. Senanayake's elder sister, Agnes Mahawalathenna, as Dorothy was not at home has given a call to the minister that she is coming with her daughter, Mangala, for her to stay for a few days in Negambo as she has involved in some ragging at the campus. A girl has fallen from upstairs and her spinal cord has got affected. Minister said Dorothy will return in the evening and let them stay in the house. He will give a call to house and advise them to provide all the facilities till Dorothy comes...

Dorothy arrived around one o 'clock and first thing she asked whether they are after lunch. She gave and affirmative answer and thanked Manika for arranging everything. She explained why she came and requested to keep Mangala for about two weeks, until university authorities probe into the accusation. Further Mangala explained all what had happened.

Dorothy said she can stay any longer, no problem. And it is not at all safer to keep her at the hostel if there is a dispute like this.

She agreed to ask IGP and her minister husband also to look into the whole matter. Dorothy advised her sister to stay tonight and leave in the morning, but she preferred to leave immediately as she has important matters to attend. She left.

Minister returned bit early and immediately he enters said "Dorothy, there is a happy news."

She followed him. "One of our contractors approached me and agreed to offer two million provided he gets the contract for the whole complex. Unless and until Cabinet approves it, I could not give him any assurance. But things seem to be pretty well. We could earn a few million rupees. But if there is any quarry or repercussion after some time, I am bit afraid."

"Don't bother about quarries and repercussions. All the ministers who get commissions have quarries. But they easily escape. When are we getting the money? So that I can start to offer 200 packets of lunch parcels to destitute people in the area on Sundays."

"Wait, wait till he brings an advance or santhosam. Probably he will come over here to discuss further and offer me something."

"You must not ask him to come over here. Take him to a hotel or any other place."

"Yes, I think that is better. Incidentally Dorothy when you were distributing 100 parcels, I noticed nearly 300 people were disappointed. They must be cursing you although you were doing a generous bit of work."

"I'll see whether I can increase the amount or adopt meticulous system once I received my quota from your santhosam."

"Yes think about it. Otherwise even you give away 500 parcels, position would be the same. Those who don't get parcels will curse you"

Minister's reply was laced with an irony.

When the Minister comes for the dinner before going to the table they discuss about the Mangala's incident. Faizal also was present.

She explained, all their batch mates at their Mars hall had an evening recreating session and they proposed to conduct ragging for the fun. Ursula who was participating at the last event where she was asked to make a striptease dance. She came to the final stage where she had to remove her knickers. She refused. They forced that she must do it. I tried to come forward and remove it. Then she starts running and saying that she will jump over the half wall. She ran towards the half wall but I ran behind and try to grab her. Meanwhile she jumped. It was the second floor. She was immediately taken to the hospital. Accusation came on me to say that I pushed her. I didn't touch her. When I went home on the following day her father came with a shot gun and threatened if something happened to her he will shoot at me. He is a ruffian guy. Amma is really scared. She didn't want me to stay at the campus. So she suggests until the authorities probe in to the matter for me to stay here.

"You will miss your lectures" Faizal comments.

"Yes Aiyya, this is my final year. I can't afford to miss a single lecture."

"You go from here. If madam and minister give permission, I'll accompany you from here to the campus until such time. It is not safer to stay at the hostel." Faizal further said.

They all agreed for the suggestion and they sat at the dinner table. Minister also arrived.

While they were having dinner they discuss further about ragging in the universities. Minister condemned the whole process "Ragging in a mild way it doesn't matter. But now it has gone too far. High time to totally ban it! It is degrading! Disgraceful!"

What is this dish? It is very tasty." Minister asked.

"I also thought of asking." Dorothy comments. She calls the bionic bitch, "Nelly, go and ask Menika to come."

The bionic bitch Nelly went to the kitchen and said that madam wanted Menika at the dining hall. "You may have put more salt to Minister's food or something like that. I am not quite sure." Menika ran briskly.

"Menika what is this?" She pointed out to the dish. "It is very tasty."

"It is a Thai recipe madam. Called pad pak Duri."

"What are the ingredients have gone into it?" Minister questioned.

"Sir, Moong beans, galangal, tofu or bean curd, durian and Thai spices"

"Oh, Durian! It is an aphrodisiac, Jack you must not eat too much!"

Faizal couldn't control his laugh. He covered his mouth and then drank a little water. "Don't worry. I'll look after myself" Minister made a quip.

Menika also returned with an uncontrollable laugh.

Mangala and Faizal were chatting after the dinner for a long time.

Nelly came and inquired, "Now madam, aren't you feel sleepy? Manika has arranged a room for you next to Sitha missy. When you feel sleepy you can go there."

"Thank you Nelly!" She said with a sultry smile.

When Menika brought two cups of tea, they got up and took the cups into their rooms.

Later at night Menika entered Faizal's room and said that she came to collect the cup if he has already drank it, Faizal got hold her. "Today your hubby has gone to the estate. You must be feeling lonely. You may stay little while with me. Is your child is still up?"

"fast asleep."

They were together for about half an hour and she left by giving him lingering kisses.

Following day, being Friday, when Faizal accompanied Sitha and Mangala back from the Campus. Sitha questioned Mangala whether she likes to go to Canada. Her daddy will select an area where she wishes to study or engage in and it is much safer for you to go from here. She expressed her willingness.

"Even I obtain BSc here, doubt whether I can get into a better position." Which suggests that her willingness to leave Sri Lanka. So Sitha agreed to contact her mama over the phone as they are also alone. Faizal revealed that he is having a cricket match on this Sunday at the SSC, with the B team and whether they like to visit. Both of them were overwhelmingly happy to attend.

When they returned home Mangala and Sitha further discussed with Mrs. Senanayake about Mangala's Canada trip and she got in touch with her mother.

Mother said she has no objection.

Then and there Sitha talked to Mangala's mother and obtained permission.

Sitha telephoned her dada and made the request. He agreed to send a letter to be forwarded to the High Commission to obtain a visit visa.

Sunday morning with Faizal they went to SSC.(Sinhalese Sports Club)

"I am inclined to familiarize with Kandyan Dancing, Faizal. Can you select a place for me?"Sitha earnestly asked.

"In Kandy area you find any number of places. I studied in several places." Mangala said.

"There was a very renowned place at Kollupitiya, Chithrasena Dancing Academy. Now they have shifted to Nawala. I'll find all details and discuss with madam too."

"O, Chithrasena's it is internationally famous!" Mangala quips. Until they reach SSC they were talking about traditional dancing in Sri Lanka.

When they stepped into the pavilion Kumari was seated in a corner table and was chatting with few of her batch mates.

Faizal directly went towards their table, greeted and introduced Mangala and Sitha. In return Kumari introduced her pals. "I am bit late, excuse me I'll go and meet the team members." He left. Sitha and Mangala didn't want to sit down although they requested. "We have to go to Odel to buy some garments. What are the other places where good garments are available?" Sitha asked.

"Try Majestic City at the Colpetty junction." Kumari informed. They said they will go and buy a few things and return.

" Okay, when you are coming you can have some refreshments here."

"All right we will be back soon."

They left.

"If they go to buy clothing, they may not return for several hours."Buela quips.

Buela, Dulci, Nirupa and Surupee were the others who were there.

" Both of them are Faizal's friends?"Nirupa asked.

" Yeah, Sitha has come from Canada. She is a dancer. Here she is reading for her doctorate on Archeology."

"Is he staying with Faizal?" Dulci questioned.

"Yeah, at the Minister of Religious Interests bungalow."

"Ah! Then shall I tell you something Kumari. Your chances to get married to Faizal may be very remote." Dulici had a sultry smile.

"I have faith on Faizal."

Kumari uttered and ordered refreshments and tea.

"You can never trust these young boys. When they are in the company of beauties, they can't control themselves." Dulci said.

"It is 100% true." Buela agreed.

"I am not going to get married to him. He is my boy friend only."

"Kumari, then why on earth you keep company with him just like your married partner."

"Well Dulci, you know very well he is my batch mate from

the time we were together in the Campus. He is my thick pal. That's all. I am very unlikely to get married to him."

"But you two are behaving just like a married couple. If you have no idea to get married, why are you associating so intimately?" Buela asked.

"Well it doesn't matter. After all in the police also we are working so together most often."

"It is true Kumari. If you have no idea to get married in future, your close friendship will be a black mark if you had to select somebody else to get married."

"Well, I have to tell who ever the unlucky fellow would be, this is only an official connection." Kumari uttered.

"But Faizal being a very handsome and robust fellow with a suitable position in the parallel-range, why don't you have an idea to make him your life partner?" Dulci asked.

"He is a Muslim and I am an upcountry Sinhala Buddhist, from an aristocratic family."

"So what's the difference?"

"He is cut" Surupee laughed loudly.

"That doesn't matter. But the point is I do not like to go against my parents under any circumstances. My parents are very orthodox. Religious minded. National conscious. Up country people. They may not like I am getting married to anybody who is not a Sinhala Buddhist."

"Love is blind Kumari. I know definitely one day you will get married to Faizal, Here the fellow has started batting. Oh my god! a sixer!" All are in the stadium started clapping.

"How smart the fellow. Still you don't want to get married to him?"

"No men, I don't want to hurt the feelings of my parents?"

"Kumari. I'll bet that you will marry Faizal and nobody else!" Buela affirmed.

"No it is definitely no. At the same time I'll see that he wants get married to anybody else."

"How can you stop that?"

"I'll see." Kumari finished her cup of tea in one gulp.

"So soon he has scored 25, just for three over." I don't mind getting married to a robust and handsome figure like Faizal. Community and Religion are immaterial to me." Buela says.

"If you want to fall out from me you may try. But I'll see he will be my boy friend throughout. He won't get married to any other soul."

"That's unfair no Kumari. He also must have the liberty. He also must plan a future, if you don't want to get married to him. You must give him the freedom to select his life partner," Dulci proposed.

"He would be my eternal boy friend. No one on earth has the right to grab him."

Kumari was firm and her response was grim.

"If Sitha and Faizal are living in the same house, don't you think they have chances to become more intimate?"

"I have full confidence on him" She ordered another cup of tea and had a big bite of a sandwich that she was munching. By that time Faizal had scored 75.Team had the tea break.

"You are a strange guy, Kumari. You are trying to stop a wind with a net. Impossible." Dulci commented while enjoying refreshments. All the other three also agreed with Dulci.

"I will send Sitha to Ravana. But Faizal will never leave me."

"Why? Have you signed an agreement?"

"Yes in our hearts."

"Hearts! That is a fallacy. Hearts can't have any decisions. Heart is a Pumping station only. There can't have any feelings or binding. Nonsense! Read the Therapy by Dr.Sripali Vaiamon. There is a valid description on relevant to the feelings in the heart."

They were chatting for a long time while watching the game.

Sitha and Mangala returned. They join the bandwagon. Kumari ordered some more eatables and cool drinks.

Sitha looked at the score board and amazed! "Oh, Faizal scored 200!"

Others looked at Kumari's face but didn't utter anything.

"You guys are waiting to see the match till the end." Kumari asked.

"No Kumari. Mangala is planning to go to Canada. We have plenty of preliminary arrangements to be made."

"It is for your place." Kumari laughed.

"Almost like."

"When is he leaving?" somebody else asked.

"Very soon!" Sitha responded. They were chatting for about fifteen minutes and left.

"If they are leaving by the car. What is the mode of transport for Faizal?" Dulci asked.

"Why are you worrying so much about Faizal? He is my baby. I'll take him."

"Sorry sorry sorry Kumari. I know he is your permanent boy. You have the right to take him anywhere you like. Shall we go to some other place for lunch? Or shall we have something from here."

"SSC lunch is very tasty. Will have from here" Surupee said.

They all decided to stay and witness the match and have the lunch at SSC.

Around four, match was over. Main team where Faizal participated had a five wicket victory. After the match they dispersed. Kumari had to provide transport to Faizal. They did not go straight to Negambo. On their way stayed at a hotel at Kandana, had dinner. Relaxed about an hour and left.

Within a week Mangala left to Canada. As Mangala has done science subjects and she has a computer skill Dr .Guptha was very happy. He had a faith that Mangala is ideal to help him in his research activities.

While having tea in the morning Mrs.Guptha said, " It is good that you came over at least as a substitute for Sitha. After Sitha left we are lonely."

"Mangala is not a substitute. She has to enter a university here or else can engage in my research activities as she is a science student with a computer literacy."

"With my British English, which we are accustomed to I may find difficulty to study in a university here."

"Oh no, that won't be a problem or else you can study for a profession that you like. The new research area where I have laid my hand is a wild goose chase.

But I firmly believe there is enough potential to achieve my objectives. I am quite sure you have the capacity to work on it. After tea let us go to the computer room I'll give an introduction. You deliberate well and let me know whether you are in a position to handle the job."

"You may have to compensate well." Mrs. Guptha suggests.

"That I'll do. It is very convenient for me if a person who is in the house could attend to it rather than an outsider. Because, even at night when you are sleeping might get a fresh idea, which you may like to experiment. Then you have to do that immediately. Otherwise the idea will get lost."

"True uncle. I like the work of this nature. I'll lay my hand." Mangala agreed.

After the breakfast, Dr .Guptha and Mangala entered the computer room.

"This is a conventional computer which you are used to. Others were specially turned out for me. These two, are quantum computers and the last one is a super computer. Their functions are slightly different. Supercomputer has the frontline of correct processing capacity. Quantum machine describes how matter and energy behave at the fundamental levels. So quantum computers harness the information –processing ability of individual atoms, photons and other elementary particles.

All interactions between particles convey not only energy but also information. You will get time to familiarize with these theories. It doesn't matter. You are a person with computer skill. To achieve my objective it will take year or two or even more. Look child! In this world, well I don't know about other worlds, the human being is unique. He could remember what he has done, what he has uttered, what he has imagined. All these have agglomerated in his brain. There are billions of dendrites in the brain which hold all these information (Ref. pps. 434,435 of The Therapy by Dr.Sripali Vaiamon)

We have to discover a method to extract all these information whenever we need through computer system."

"If the person can't remember certain things?"

"Good interruption. You must ask questions where ever there are doubts, these information are there in his brain. Not completely vanished. We have to excavate them. And then transliterate to the computer. Language is immaterial. Any language we should be able to put it to the computer and computer will translate into English, French or other languages. Even a person suffered from Alzheimer disease, we would be able to excavate and sharpen the blurred information. They are all in particles and in wave forms. All interactions between particles in the universe convey not only energy but also information. Computer is a machine that process information. The method of quantum simulation is direct and efficient. So through these quantum computers I am, confident I can hit at the target."

"Although this would be something new, the theory is not altogether new. Isn't it?"

"You are very clever. I appreciate that. The notion that waves are made of particles is fairly old. The sound is made of waves has been known since Pythagoras. Evan Buddha has articulated that MANO PUBBHA, MANOMAYA. Brain is crucial. Mind is in the brain. Mind is the matrix of all matters. Everything from about three years after the birth that recorded in the cells of the brain would be there. We have to unearth them and receive in wave form and then could be transliterated in the computer.

You concentrate on this and try to grasp what I elaborated. Let's discuss at length when time permits. Now I have to report to the hospital. You wait here and study. See you."

He tapped at her shoulder and left.

Little later Mrs.Guptha visited the computer room to see on what Mangala is being engaged. "This is very interesting aunty! I like to develop my computer skill with the help of uncle. I am really interested."

"Okay then you go ahead, I am going to the Orchard."

"I like to visit the Orchard and the Winery too, aunty!"

"Okay, then get ready and come with me."

She accompanied Mangala and visited the Orchard. She asked question after question and learn a lot about growing apples and how apple ciders are being brewed etc. There she met a girl who had visited the orchard. She had a hockey stick in her hand.

"Where are you playing hockey?" She casually asked.

"In the school." She replied and introduced herself. So did Mangala.

On her way home she told Mrs.Guptha, that she is quite good at hockey and desire to see a game where they play here.

She agreed to take her and said there is an interesting hockey match at the Toronto Hockey Club today. It is ice hockey. If she is interested can go in the evening when her husband returns. She agreed.

In the evening when Dr .Guptha returns they visited the hockey match.

"It is very strenuous uncle."

"Yes it is. You must have a very good experience on skating to do ice hockey."

" How am I to learn skating uncle?"

"There is a place close by, if you are interested I can take you there." Mrs.Guptha responded.

"I like aunty. After coming over to Canada, I must learn something that is popular in Canada, which is not available in Sri Lanka. Although I have seen snow sports, skating in movies, I did not get a chance to observe live. This is the first opportunity. I got an inspiration!" She uttered in surprise like a baby.

"We will take you Mangala to watch all the ice-games." Doctor was highly pleased on her enthusiasm.

"If you are interested on ice-games, including ice-hockey, first thing you have to learn skating. That is the primary step." Mrs. Guptha articulated.

"Where am I got to learn skating aunty?"

"There is a Club close by, and they have training classes for beginners. Mostly children, but no restriction, you can join." Mrs.Guptha said.

" I like. But this may requires lot of money. I'll speak to my mom tomorrow morning."

"Money is no problem child. I'll take you there tomorrow morning."

She was highly pleased. Following day they visited Toronto Hockey Club. She was enrolled to the beginners' class. The Instructor entrusted was a young German youth,
Rudolf Wilhelm.

He said one-hour classes are available three days a week at 8.oo in the morning. She must come with a hockey helmet. Face masks as she is a beginner. Leather skates with laces are preferred. Mittens or gloves and snow pants as required. We will first teach you standing, stepping forward and then gliding. It won't be much difficult." He said with a glowing smile.

They agreed to purchase all the required tools and meet tomorrow.

Following day morning there was a call from Sitha to Mangala. But dad who answered said she has gone to skating classes. Mother has gone to the orchard. They had a chat for a long time and Sitha informed that they are planning to visit Sitha Amman temple and another cave where Ravana supposed to have written one of his books.

"That is off Nuwara Eliya. I have been to Sitha Amman temple but not to the other place. You visit the place and let me know all the details. I'll come over there in a few weeks time. Now I have to go to the hospital. I'll talk to you later. They bid bye and wound up.

Mangala was very happy. "Within a day I learned how to glide on ice. Isn't that strange aunty?"

"O it is very good." Doctor appreciated. "You did not fall?" He asked bit sarcastically.

"About thrice! But I didn't give up. My instructor is excellent." She uttered with a pride.

They had this conversation while having dinner.

Dr. Guptha realized Mangala is a very enthusiastic girl

and she will pick up his computer activities too within a short span of time although there is no short cut for the specific research.

"Madam, I spoke to that chap at the bungalow, Suraweera. He said he could accompany us. He advised us to come over to the bungalow in the evening, so that following day early morning could depart and visit several places relevant to Ramayana.

He further said that there is an Upasaka who knows much about these things who is living closer to his hut where he was residing."

"Yeah, I know that. When are you expecting to go?"

"We can leave here after lunch on Saturday"

"You and Sitha alone?"

"No Kumari is coming with us."

"Ah, that is good. Sitha is very anxious. You go ahead with the arrangement. I'll inform Simon at the bungalow and talk to Suraweera too."

"Thanks madam."

Saturday around six in the evening they arrived at the bungalow. After dinner they went out for a walk although they felt pinch cold as winter wind.

"O I am shivering. But may not be cold at all to Sitha?"

"Not at all!"

They visited the town. Relaxed at the Park for about half an hour and returned.

Simon the bungalow keeper had arranged two rooms for three of them One room with the queens bed for two ladies and a single room for Mr.Faizal Mohamud.

"Why a separate room for you? Is it because you are a Muslim? Come here man." She dragged him. "We three can manage in this queen size bed. It is big enough." Kumari dropped down at the centre.

"I'll be in the left side." Sitha suggests.

"That's good even if you fall it will be on this thick carpet." Kumari said amusedly.

Faizal went to the other end. So Kumari was sandwiched comfortably. She started chatting and joking.

"Now let's sleep. Sitha turned to a side. Kumari turned to the other side and with her back pushed her. Sitha was rolled on to the carpet.

"I am sorry Sitha" Kumari pretended.

"That's Okay. I didn't get hurt."

Faizal came running right round the bed and raised her "I'll get into the centre. You go to the other side." Faizal proposed and laid down at the centre.

"Then you will be like a rose between two thorns." Kumari uttered.

"Thorn between two roses" Sitha corrected.

"Naturally, he has a blunt thorn." Kumari said sarcastically and put her hand over his chest. Faizal put his fingers over Sitha's palm and pressed to the bed so that Kumari didn't see.

"My hands long to caress you."Kumari pressed his ear.

"Now without a mum let's sleep. He started purposely groaning.

"Why are you groaning today?" She turned to his side, "Okay, Okay now let's sleep without snoring." Kumari put her leg also over his legs. Just to show her intimacy and indirectly to tease Sitha.

Following day morning after breakfast they started the journey. About 5 km off they arrived at Sitha Amman temple.

It was a beautifully decorated Hindu temple. Sitha earnestly watched all the nook and corners and sculptors which were beautifully built in order to attract tourists. She asked various questions from the Poosari, the priest in charge. He agreed to take them out and show where Hanuman took rest at the Asoka Forest after the war. There were two foot marks.

Then they visited the opposite bank where Sitha had bathe and meditated. He further said at Ramboda there is Sri Bhkatha Hanuman Temple and Divrumpola where Sitha sworn.

"Faizal shall we go" Kumari suggests as Sitha will take far too much of time to watch all the places which are supposed to be associated with Rama's legend.

"I don't mind but Sitha seems to be interested."

"But tell her according to former Director of Archaeology all these are falsely created views and must not take so seriously. He has expressed these are new-fanged ideas and better to left alone."

They started their journey again. They went to Katumana and from there veered into a bumpy road and in half an hour's time reached the place that Suraweera suggested. When they arrived at Upasaka's hut Suraweera suggests,

"Then let's go to meet the Upasaka. We can get advice from him. He is a well educated man. Read horoscopes and quite good at astrology, well versed in Ayurvedic medicine, good at palmistry too."

"Then let's go there."

Kumari evinced an interest.

"Fortunately Upasaka is in." Suraweera said when he saw Upasaka at his table. He introduced them to Upasaka and gave a brief description. They were anxious to see the cave where Ravana wrote his books.

"Sitha!" He repeated her name several times. "I like to see your palm child."

Sitha immediately stretched her hand. "You are very fortunate. But take care from whom you associate. You have inborn talents in various fields. You would be able to understand Ravana. Let us go to the forest at 12. There is about half an hour more."

"What are all these old books?"

Faizal was inquisitive. "Are those Ravana's books?"

"No, no! I don't have any Ravana's book. But some of these are dealt on Ravana. Some are on astrology and medicine. I have a very precious paper miraculously received. It is a Ravana's powerful Mantra. If a person, if fortunate enough, when learn by heart and committed to the memory he can become invisible."

"Can't I have it?" Kumari was extremely anxious.

"Well, I don't give it to each and every one and more over if I am to give to any one, it has to be given on a Nekath day at an auspicious time. Today there is no auspicious time although it is a good day. Very unfortunate child! If you come on some other day we can see whether there is a possibility." Upasaka was bit suspicious and further ordered Suraweera,

"Okay. Suraweera give them with some water to wash their hands and faces before entering the forest."

Suraweera went out and brought water in a bucket and poured into their hands to wash themselves.

After that Upasaka accompanied the three and left to the forest. Suraweera stayed behind.

"There is a black cat guarding the cave, but don't get scared. He will leave when we go."

Upasaka said when they approached the opening of the cave a black panther looked at them and slowly disappeared. Cave entrance was half way covered with creepers. Inside was bit dark. But Faizal had a big flash light with him. He suspiciously took it as they have to trudge in the forest. Beyond the entrance it was pitch- dark. Faizal flashed the torch.

"Don't do that. We don't know the extent of this tunnel. It is extremely dark. No one can go. There may be snakes but fortunately not a single bat unlike all such caves." He lighted coconut oil lamps and a bundle of incense and fixed in a tin vase. The cloying smell of incense drifting in the cave was pleasant.

"Let's go out to see the cat."

Kumari dragged Faizal and came out. Upasaka started to mutter Incantation mantra.

"Oh, Cat is there. It is a black panther, dangerous, let's go in."

"Wait I'll take a photograph." Faizal had a camera but when he focused the panther disappeared. They went in." Where is Sitha?" Sitha is not to be seen. Faizal got bewildered, panic and puzzled. He focused the flash light into the tunnel. Upasaka got upset. He stopped his mantra and started calling "Sitha, Sitha, Sitha where are you?"

Where are you? Faizal got so scared and tried to go into the tunnel. Upasaka didn't allow him. He started his mantra again. Faizal kept on flashing the light to the tunnel.

He didn't know what to do. He thought if Suraweera would have come with him he would have gone into the tunnel. After all he has to be responsible for Sitha.

He also started calling Sitha, and kept on focusing the light. He got unbelievably scared. Kept on flashing the light until the battery gets totally drained.

"Let's go out a bit to see outside."

Kumari dragged him and came out. Look around. But no sign! They went in "O my god, Sitha is there! Where on earth you disappeared? I got so scared." By that time Sitha has come out with a golden style which Ravana had utilized to script his books on palm leaves. (A sort of a metal pen) On Upasaka's advice she kept it inside her hand bag and Upasaka had asked her not to show it to anybody or talk about it.

Faizal threw his hand around her neck, hold tightly and warned not to go anywhere without telling him.

"I am sorry Faizal. I don't know what had happened to me. All of a sudden I was in a chamber, a well lit chamber. There was an elderly lady and two young girls. They treated me very well. Placed a dot on my forehead, gave some syrup to drink. Gave me this metal stick and asked me to preserve it." So with that I came out. I didn't was there even a minute."

"Nonsense! You came after a long time. My flash light completely drained. May be about half an hour."

"Is that so! I didn't realize."

"Now let's go children without talking much about what had happened. Guard your tongues." Upasaka called them and they came out and out of the forest. Didn't tell even Suraweera who was waiting till they come. They thanked Upasaka and got into the car with Suraweera and drive fast. They didn't utter a word until they reach the bungalow.

"I must have a shower" Sitha proposed immediately she entered the bungalow.

"I also must have a wash." Kumari went inside the room along with Sitha.

While Sitha is having a shower, Kumari had a body wash.

"What happened Sitha?"
She asked.

"I don't know Kumari. This seems to be a mystery. That's why perhaps Upasaka advised not to talk about it, let's keep our mouths shut. I don't want to tell even Mrs. Senanayake and the Minister. There must be having something, something which I can't articulate. It was a mystery. It was a mystery!"

They had lunch without much uttering and thanked

Suraweera and Simon and returned home. Simon had kept in the boot a basket of flowers to be handed over to madam.

Same day night Sitha phoned up her dada and explained all what had happened. He too was eager to fly over to Sri Lanka and pay a visit to the spot. Minister also it seems very unhappy these days as his suggestion on World religious complex is likely to be bogged down as the President is not in good mood, perhaps because her term is almost over. So in couple of week's time I am planning to visit Sri Lanka. He repeatedly asked to keep the mystic object in a safe place.

Mangala who was very eager to practice ice hockey, requested Rudolf to give her a preliminary training on the game. He accompanied her to a club where school girls were practicing ice hockey.

He introduced her to some of the participants after their game was over. With two of them Rudolf entered the arena. A hockey stick was borrowed from the club for Mangala. He instructed her how to hold the stick and play.

With the help of the two girls she started playing. She could not glide fast and control herself as a result she was fallen down several times. But gained little experience. Rudolf assured to come again and train her. He accompanied her for tea with the other two girls. There he reveled that he is a computer technician and at the moment involved in quantum computer calculations. If they are interested he can accompany them to his office and demonstrate.

They agreed to visit some other day but Mangala was anxious to come.

He explained Mangala what is quantum computer and its working system starting from the bit. She picked up a fairly good knowledge but she admits the processing is very complicated and at the moment she is practicing the mechanics with her uncle, Dr. Guptha, a Gynecologist at the Peel Memorial hospital. He was highly satisfied and anxious to meet him one day.

When Mangala returned home she explained everything to Doctor and Mrs.Guptha.

"I like to meet the boy. He perhaps would be useful for our research activities."

"I thought the same uncle."

"Can't you invite him over here on a free day."

"I think if I suggest he will come."

"Next Sunday morning I don't have anything specific. If he is free ask him to come around 11'oclock."

"O, then he can have lunch with us and go."

Mrs.Guptha suggests.

"That's not a bad idea." Doctor agreed.

"I'll suggest him uncle."

When Mangala conveyed the message, he was really delightful and accepted the invitation.

Sitha, although Upasaka asked her not to show anyone the golden style she mysteriously received, she felt it is unfair if she do not show it to Minister and madam.

"Aunty I have something to show you and uncle. But it should be a dead secret. Shall I call uncle?" Sitha suggests while Mrs. Senanayake was dressing up to go for a function.

"Yeah you may call him. He must be reading the headlines of morning papers at the foyer."

She went and accompanied him. When he arrived, she showed them the golden style and explained how she got it and the advice Upasaka gave to her not to show to others and talk about it. "How can I keep it as a secret to uncle and aunty?"

They got bit astonished. If he advised thus, there ought to be something. KeepKeep this safely and do not tell anybody else. This is something very obscure. I cannot imagine.

When I return from the Parliament will discuss about this in detail. Now you go and keep it in a safe place."
Minister advised her.

Minister just could not imagine and the historical value of that article. Mrs. Senanayake also was dumfounded. "If you do not have a safe place to keep it, I can keep it in the iron safe." She proposed.

"But Dorothy it is better to keep in a place where she is and suggests, "You keep in your closet drawer but see that it is always locked."

"I'll do that uncle. Nobody will come and pull out my things."

As discussed, Rudolf called over at Dr.Das Guptha's apartment at the condominium. When he rang the bell, Mangala came and opened the door. "Good morning Sir, come in." She called him with a thousand watt smile. They seated and had a short chat. Then Doctor came out. Mangala immediately introduced her trainer as Mr. Rudolf Wilhelm to Doctor. Mrs. Judy Guptha also came out. He was introduced to Mrs.Guptha too, and after a short chat she went towards the kitchen. Little while later Lee brought tea with pot and cups in a tray. While they were sipping tea Doctor briefed on his project. "My plan is, rather my dream is to read what is stored in some one's brain even from child hood. I don't want to have any electrode net put on to one's head. Once I send a SMS message to excavate necessary information from someone's brain which had been recorded exactly in the tiny cells in the brain of any person. In all vertebrates the brain located in the head where in the cerebral cortex there are roughly fifteen to thirty three billions neurons. These neurons communicate with one another by means of axons which carry signal pulses called action potentials. Memories rest on those. So we have to combine the cell phone technology, nano technology and quantum technology to excavate these memories in a human brain. Shell we go to the computer room. So that you will get a better picture of the whole set up." They all got up and entered the computer room. These hardware although look like PCs, they are not. This big one is a super computer, exact replica in miniature size of the Tianhe-1A computer of China. The other two are IBM designs. One is different from the other.

We can get the name and address of a person, his present position, his status, body temperature, height, weight and shape. His blood sample, rhythm of the blood flows and finally the shape and the picture will display in the super computer. Then the 1st quantum computer will register his language, pose a few questions. He will answer the questions and answers reflect on the screen of the Super computer. You will welcome the person and raise one or two questions. His answers emerge from his brain and appear on the screen. Thereafter you ask required questions, which you can repeat if necessary. To hit at this target we have to think and think and work out a better system to be adopted. You may not know how long it will take. If the time permits, you may experiment it several times."

"Now, Japanese have discovered a new Super computer.

They have named it as "K." It has the capability to make 8.2 quadrillion calculations per second." It was from Rudolf.

"I am really not interested on the speed. But the methodology and the accuracy are paramount." Doctor commented.

"This computer pushed back the previous number one, Tianhe-1A Super computer, at the National Supercomputing Centre in Tianjin, China, to second place. It has been housed in 672 cabinets filled with system boards."

"colossal! Science is ever developing."

"You never know what and what things will discover in near future."

"unimaginable! But the strange concept would be however those discoveries scientifically sound, philosophically would be defective."

"Would it be?"

"From religious point of view, it would be!"

They both together discuss while Doctor opted to come out to read the morning papers.

Minister Senanayake was thoroughly upset as the President was not in favor of cutting down coconut trees in the estate Minister proposed or even in any other place.

Minister is eager to get 250 acres of land from densely populated area. "You may have to find a barren land from somewhere to start your project and funds have to be collected from business people in the country or elsewhere provided your bill approves the Cabinet. My term will be over by 2005. So I don't want the present Cabinet to approve this .Why don't you wait till the Presidential election is over. Then whoever the President elected will approve this. No one will go against religious matters. Wait until the new President elects. She uttered in a lethargic mood. Minister seems to be upset. He was skeptical whether the project will be bogged down. He had no other alternative. But compelled to wait.

After the Presidential election was over, the new President appoints a new Cabinet. Fortunately Mr. Senanayake was reappointed as the Minister of Religious Interests. He was very happy as he is having a broad plan to be presented to the New Cabinet on the very first day.

Well he did it. No one make any comment against it and it was unanimously accepted but it was imperative to present at the Parliament with details and expenditure involved for approval and if approved it had to be presented to the Cabinet for final approval.

Well after it was approved by the Parliament and subsequently it came for final discussion with the President and obtained the final approval. President's Secretaries and Advisers were present.

"I have already got in touch with some contractors."

"Oh no! You are being a well experienced MP you should know the procedure. You have to select the venue make the estimate with the breakdown call for tenders by your department. Then let them select the tenders. Not necessarily the lowest. The best tenders according to the views of the tender board. Once you decide the venue and then plan how to get funds. Government is almost bankrupted after the 30-year civil war. Whatever resources available have to be invested on productive projects. Religions can wait. There is no hurry. Why, do you want to go to heaven very soon?" President asked sarcastically.

"No Sir, this I planned long ago during the last President's tenure. So I am eager to start as early as possible."

"Well where are you intending to put this up?"

"It should be in a densely populated area. Then only people will patronize the place often."

"You mean in Colombo?"

"Somewhere close by in the western province. I thought of having it in Chilaw."

"It has to be away from Colombo not in a densely populated area. We can't possibly spare any land from such areas. Select a barren land. You required about 250 acres according to your plan. I can allocate from Suriyawewa, in Hambanthota, where a massive stadium for cricket has been mapped out. You think about it and let me know prior to map out your preliminary arrangements. Well gentleman, we may approve this tentatively. Okay." So it was approved.

Minister was just like a crest fallen cock after a cockfight. He didn't want to argue further. After all he got the approval.

So he decided to meet the President unofficially to enlighten him further on his intention and proper plan. He got an appointment and visited him at Temple trees.

After arguing, rather discussing for a long time he finally said he wishes to see sufficient people always in the place like Tooth Relic Temple or the Kelaniya Temple or Kochchikade St. Anthony's church where devotees patronize often. Otherwise spending so much of money is not worth President."

"Don't worry minister that area will be like Colombo in ten years time. There would be a massive, busy harbour an

Airport and factories and various other ventures. A massive religious complex as you have planned is very essential.

I sincerely thanked you for coming out with such a useful and fruitful vision. To be franked I am not favor in cutting down a single coconut tree.

Densily populated areas have to be utilized for other productive ventures, and moreover Government can't levy any expenditure on unproductive ventures such as religions. So it is imperative you find money from elsewhere. I will give you an excellent tip. Make your suggestion to foreign countries. Such as England. Get them to build a replica of St.Paul's Church. Get Thailand to build a replica of Great Emerald Temple. Propose Saudi Arabia to construct great Holy Mosque Mecca. Al-Masjid-al Haram, the holiest place of Islam. St. Peter's Basilica in Vatican, Borobudur in Java. Get South Korea to build a replica of one of their great Mahayana temples. Get China to build a replica of their great temple in Beijing, Guanji Buddha Temple and replicas of such great Temples, Mosques, Kovils and Churches of the world. Then this will be the greatest Religious Complex in the whole world. You will get a big pride building such a vast Religious Complex in this little island. People will flock from all over. I'll allocate you 500 acres. They can engage 50% of their labor forces. They can employ their own people to maintain these places. We have no burden.

Not only our locals even people of foreign countries then patronize this place. And there will have ample tourists." President was in enthusiastic mood.

"Excellent idea Sir. Your vision is great. I'll work out on it. Thank for your suggestions. Good bye." He left.

On his way back he was contemplating on President's massive proposal. He thought definitely he will earn laurels once the project is accomplished. Only disadvantage is he would not be able earned a satisfactory commission. But that can forgo if he could build a world religious complex as suggested by the President. It would be a great task. If we do that prior to other countries he is definitely earn a great reputation.

Immediately he arrived home without delay he discussed about the proposed venture. He thanked President for his unprecedented vision. He visualized it again and again as a local politician. But repented as only hitch that he is not in a position to make sufficient commission on the line he and his wife contemplated.

"I am happy that you avoided getting my property at Chilaw and don't bother you can get commissions from other minor constructions. Even my program will bog down I am sure. He will propose to have it in Suriyawewa. I don't mind putting a Khajuraho there after about five years' time. But the first one I must put up in the western province. I'll convince President on this."

"What will happen if he is not agreeable to such an obscene project? He will reject"

"This is to enlighten human weaknesses. He won't reject. First I must have a discussion on this with my well wishers."

"As a matter of fact I wanted you to promote this idea through your learned friends. President's wife is also an educated woman. You can get her views prior to approach the President.

On the advice of the Minister, She summoned her well to do women folks for a lunch and a discussion at her palace.

"Well, I'll brief what is in my mind. When I visited Khajuraho Art Museum in India I got the inspiration to open up a similar art gallery for the sake of our people.

Of course it should be opened to girls and boys above eighteen or at the first instance, should be confined to married couples only. Ancient Indian people who obtained advice from sages constructed these museum probably based on Vathsaliya's Kama Sutra and depicted erotic sculptures displaying various methods of sexualities for ordinary folks to get the idea and educate themselves on mutual living to sustain a happy married life. Unless they know various arts on sexology they cannot achieve satisfaction and their life become dreary and boring. Consequently they had to live an unsuccessful life with frustration. If they know various techniques they can enjoy the life so long as they live or according to church advocates live unto death. Now we must help our people living in this third world country, mostly village folks, to live a happy life. Without force them to get divorced or go in search of paramours and mess up their married life. I thought of having similar but advanced type of an art gallery with video pictures to expose separately for males and females who are in adult age. This is the idea of my project. I like to have your genuine views.

Ancient sages did all these for the benefit of the mankind. They wrote books on medicines, astrology, religion and various other subjects without attending to any university. It is on their advice and specific instruction kings built places like Kahjuraho, with erotic architecture. Not with any vulgar idea as such. They are meaningful. They are extremely beneficial to human beings. Now of course in the developed countries they teach sex education to school children. Adults have no scientific knowledge on sex in our countries. Consequently most of married couples lead arid life with frustration. Some ended up with divorce others live eternally in frustration. The sex is something prime important in human life. Even most of the educated people have not considerably realized. Some think it as obscene, vulgar but fundamentally if you think deep you will realize there is nothing vulgar in it. It is the cultures in different countries have made it obscene. Otherwise it is something natural. Why human beings were formed as male and female. Procreation is one aspect. More than what they achieve from their day to day life, sexual fulfillment is paramount.

To sustain a happy married life sex is the prime objective. When I visited Khajuraho in India, I asked myself. Why these people have built these erotic sculptures. Was It because of their sadistic ideas? No. It is with more deep thinking. To sustain the human life man and woman should get married, procreate children and primarily they must lead a happy married life. For that sexual experience is a prime requirement. They should know the science of sexology. Then only they can live happily.

Most of our men and women who get married have no scientific sexual knowledge at all.

First and foremost they must have a good understanding on sexual life. They can't learn that in schools or universities. So we have to help them with a good motive, as some will feel it is bit vulgar we have to confine the exhibition to adults only. No celibate people should be entertained. So this we have to project more scientifically as these are not freely available for people to watch and gain a knowledge.

In computers, prone films are there but all can't afford for those luxuries. We must have simple project to fulfill the desires of the general public. All projects, sequences will be projected in video form. So we must plan how this should be done. Most of you are being well to do people have these stuffs individually experienced.

We must provide this opportunity to public in a most suitable way with a clear motive. This is what I envisage now. Let us discuss pros and cons to arrive at a decision. If we can't arrive at a decision on one day, no harm we can have discussions for several days and obtain if necessary technical and professional opinions from experts. Now I will open the discussion to the forum."

Dorothy concluded.

Mrs. William Bochs opened the forum and thanked Mrs. Senanayake for excellent views which she feels very essential for our third world country. But this also I must stress in advanced countries like America, France, Britain married lives haven't become bed of roses with scientific knowledge on the sex. They also have dissatisfactions, arguments fights and ultimately divorces. So knowledge and familiarization along are not criteria to lead a satisfactory married life. There are enough family councils in the country with all that there are discrepancies and had evinced good results too. So no harm try the possibility of experimenting Mrs. Senanayake's philosophy as Khajuraho." She gave a pause.

"Thanks! Mrs. Bochs, let others also project their views."Mrs. Senanayake requested.

Mrs.Thirunanasundaram got up, "Well I am not in coherence with the suggestion. We are of course as descent women do not like to expose our sexual behavior in public. Even as married people we do that quietly in a room, often at night, when nobody is in close by. That is because we do not like to expose these affairs…"

She was disturbed. "Mrs.Thirunanasundaram has not fully grasped what we talk about. It is not what Dorothy proposed. We do sexual affairs not openly as descent women, but what we suggest that we should educate married people to have sex with a full understanding. They should familiarize with all techniques, otherwise it may become boring. Ultimately their married life too becomes boaring, which lead to several negative consequences.

No proper satisfaction they will gain. For that we have to enlighten them with new techniques and proper methods. 75% of all couples have problems in their sex life. Higher number of marriages have stress and ultimately break up. Marriage is actually a physical and mental health issue. Relationship satisfaction and sexual satisfaction may not be the same for every couple. Frequently cuddling or kissing also enhance happiness in their relationship. If they can find ways and means to keep up the happiness constantly for a greater period of their married life that could be treated as happy marriage."

"Absolutely, that is what I intended." Dorothy interrupted. "Her brain is buzz with bright ideas. Others too contribute with such views our attempt will become fruitful. So that with actualities in the form of moving visuals we could educate them with proper sexual methods, energetic love making, sensitive holding, cuddling which will enable them to have pleasurable sex which bring utmost satisfaction to both of them. That is the culture of the marriage.I have brought a few video clips with actualities plus life size cartoon images with which you will get a proper understanding." She manipulates the projector.

"These are really exciting. But could we exhibit them in Public?"

"It won't be strictly a public affair as such. It will strictly confine to married couples or adults, say above 18 and would be exhibited in an enclosed cubicle.Now let me elaborate it further.For this we have to build a circuler hall to exhibit all the visuals for two hours. 120 minutes.There will have two rows for males and femals that they do not see each other.There will have 60 cubicles in each side where in each cubicle 12 people could accommodate.They can be there and watch only for two minutes.Police officer will follow them in a passage. In every two minutes a light will flash and a bell rings.Then the door to the next cubicle will open and they shoud move in.Police officer will follow them up to the very end of their journey. In the passage there will have wash rooms.If any body wants to go their tickets will get punched with the cubicle number. When they return they have to go into the same cubicle.In the 5oth cubicle tea,coffee,cool drinks and chocolates or cookies will be served free of charge.Once they complete their journey both males and females arrive at a shopping complex where various sexual gadgets,condoms,medications for impotents etc. available.They could buy a BLESSING IN DISGUISE for a concession rate.Each adult when produce the ID will get a ticket for Rs.15. A nominal fee.Married people if they produce their marriage certificate will be charged only Rs.10. Always a doctor, nurse and electrician is available in addition to security officers.

Vedeo clips and cartoons will be provided weekly by a Netherland Company.All the demonstration and lectures would be in trilingual,that is in Sinhala, Tamil and English. This is the first time in the world going to set up an exhibition of this nature.Our little island will get a credit on this."Mrs. Senanayake concluded.

"Sexuality is culturally a taboo subject." Mrs. Wilson ignites a controversy.

"Then the marriage also should be a culturally a taboo. Because immediately after the wedding they go for honeymoon for the sex. Where there is absolutely no restriction from any quarter, culturally or otherwise."Mrs. Anderson commented.

"Exactly!'Sexuality is a part of nature of any human being." Somebody says.

"You are entitled for any comment for or against." remarked Mrs. Senanayake.

"Sex is life affirming. It is certainly worth considering."

"In married life husband ought to love their wives as they love their own bodies. For this they must have a proper understanding. They must be familiar with their anatomy and study how to sustain their married life with fulfillment, with utmost satisfactory. Then only they can lead a contended married life as church advocates unto death."Mrs.Bochs affirmed.

"Christian idea of marriage is based on Christ's words that a man and wife are to be regarded as a single organism. Similar to a violin. Violin and bow are two parts but consider as one instrument. So their bonding together forever is a prime principle in married life. If we can promote that philosophy with an attractive theory or method we have to do that with good intention. The project Mrs. Senanayake thrown to us is very valuable and substantive for the sake of happy married life of our brothers and sisters for which we must give our consent completely. In this regard I wish to quote few lines from a book by Dr.Eric Braverman, an anti-aging expert from the US, with apology to him; he says that sex not only raises hormone levels of a man but can also boost his metabolism, brain function, heart health and immunity. Further he says, eating brown rice can help combat sexual coldness, while avocadoes might increase capacity for pleasure. Orgasms are brought to fight infection-increasing the number of infection-fighting cells by up to 20%. The greater sexual activity in older men might protect them against prostate cancer. Along with our instructions on sexuality we must provide them with these information for them to lead a happy married life. " Concluded Mrs. Bochs.

"Thank you Mrs. Bochs. We need not take any vote as such here. I may have to face a battle to get this approved with the President, Ministers and the Government. So I'll proceed the matter with them. What I primarily need the support of my colleagues who always come forward with me for my philanthropist activities. After all we human are always likely to make blunders in the process of our social work. Let's thrust this and see the result. I must thank all of you for participating in this discussion. Now let's disperse for our lunch. She wound up the meeting.

The meeting was adjourned for the lunch.

Mrs. Senanayake got an appointment with the President and went over to Temple Trees one hour early. She thought she must have a chat with the first lady who is also an educated person and being a responsible mother could get her opinion first.

"Isn't this something illegal as to show in public?" She got amazed and bewildered for Mrs. Senanayake, being a wife of a responsible minister to come out with such an idea.

"We have to think this deeply madam. Even when the proposal for family council came up, I am sure learned people must have got bewildered. Or even advanced Europeans may not have agreed. When they thought of introducing sex education to school children may have had the same amazement. But after discussing pros and cons agreed with high expectations. Now even for lower class children sex matters are being taught. On the contrary for adults, particularly for married couples for their satisfactory living without a break ups in the marriages this is a something very essential.

Take for an example after all the pomposity of a marriage, couple leaves with lot of fun and frolic for honeymoon. For what purpose? Just to have sex. The preliminary event for them to build up their married life. It is the fundamental step to lead their married life. Is there anything bad about it, although no one openly discuss. It is the most important thing in their married life. They have the pleasure. They have the fun. The same pleasure, they must continue to have throughout their life. We must encourage them to keep it up. That's why we have to see both parties more scientifically, methodically educated. We must put them into a family university, provide them with essential education, awards, and degrees. They will be then fully contended."

"She had a hearty laugh! But there is something in what

you say. I fully agree. But I don't know whether President approves this. He has to be responsible to the country. Don't you know the Opposition! This is enough for them to shout for months."

Then she thought there is something valid in what she said. She decided to have a preliminary discussion with President and immediately had an official discussion with the Leader of the Opposition.

She met the President. He listened to her well. Didn't raise any objection. But he said he will appoint a commission consists of three Professors.

They are supposed to be the educated people in a country and if they approve I'll discuss with the cabinet and Okay it tentatively to conduct for one year. Depend on the outcome you may continue." He wound up.

Then on the same day she got an appointment with the Leader of the Opposition.

"Yes, in this third world countries marriage is strictly a traditional affair. But beyond that they know nothing. Get married. Procreate children. Almost like in animal kingdom. There after live a boring life. As they are bound to live together, they just live. I praise your concept. It is very fruitful idea. You put it to the President, I am sure he will approve this on the basis that you planned to exhibit the whole process to adult audience. I wish full success for your venture."

Mrs. Senanayake thanked him for his understanding and left. She conveyed everything to the minister immediately returned from the Opposition Leader's office.

When they were having dinner, Faizal commented, "Madam, this is coming within the ambit of law. Even you exhibit in enclosed cubicles or halls to the public, invariably it will be a public show. So legally there are restrictions."

Minister advised, "You consult our departmental lawyer. Otherwise it will have bad reflection on me too."

She normally doesn't want to postpone and drag anything. That is her nature. On the following day morning she met Mr.Amarabandu, Legal Officer attached to the Ministry of Religious Interests. She clearly demonstrated her entire program and requested him to carefully look into legal restrictions. Amarabandu was thorough with the subject. He said absolutely nothing to worry madam. These do not come under Public Performance Act. As such, explicit sex that is neither violent nor degrading nor dehumanizing is not obscene. As you have focused your project for married couples and to exhibit for males and females separately This do not interfere even with the envisaged Obscene Publication Act to be introduced by the Authorities.

Even if you consider young boys and girls above 18 and exhibit for two genders separately there will have no objection.

Moreover your objective is to educate the public who are in the suitable age groups to lead a satisfactory life, with thorough understanding of their married life. If you are exhibiting in an enclosed hall separately for males and females, law has no objection. You can go ahead if you get the formal approval of the Government.Moreover you know madam,In Vienna,in Austria has now opened up the world's first International sex college,where authorities allow boys and girls above 16,who would be in marriageable age near future to study on applied sexuality.With emphasis on how to be true and better lovers.Then they learn caressing techniques and avoid unwanted pregnancies. You know madam all human beings are subject to some kind of sexual weaknesses.There are modern medications available to attack the root cause without any known side effects.There are men and women with plenty of weakneses which some of them do not want to come out with.They hide their weaknesses and suffer silently.Life then become dreary and dull.Ultimately marriages will ruin prematurely or lead to a divorce.Some have depressed libido,Exhaustion after coitus,Lack of vitality, General debility,infertility,Erectile dysfunction,premature ejaculation,seminal debility,impotency,weak and tiny sex organ,unable to give satifaction to a woman.For all these human weaknesses there are very effective therapys.But must not beguiled by quacks.Your project could provide them with sufficient information and better opinions.Pl.go ahead with your project. I wish you a brilliant success."

"Thank you so much your excellent advices and information Mr.Amarabandu.Those would be very very useful to me.Thanks once again."

"You are welcome madam."

She thanked Mr.Amarabandu and then and there conveyed his opinion to the husband.

"Then you have nothing to worry about but meet the Panel appointed by the President…Incidentally I have a happy news to you Dorothy. I have written to twenty countries about my religious complex. All of them have highly praised and written to me. Eight of them willing to start without delay replicas of their highly praised religious domains. England prepared to build a replica of West Minister Abbey, Vatican, and St. Peter's Basilica. Germany, Colniche Dome. France, Notre dame Cathedral of Paris, China, Jade Buddhist Temple in Shanghai, Thailand, Emerald Buddhist Temple in Bangkok, Indonesia, Istiqbal great Mosque in Jakarta. I immediately informed the President. He is highly pleased. He said he will then and there inform the Land Department and Construction Division to allocate 500 acres of land at Suriyawewa, closer to the Cricket Stadium. However I must go and personally meet him this evening and have a pleasant chat."

"I wish you the best of luck Jack." Dorothy was equally happy.

Dr. Guptha was anxious to visit Sri Lanka particularly to visit the cave where Sitha got the golden style. He telephoned Sitha and informed her in two weeks time he is coming to Sri Lanka. Mangala is not so particular as she is very interested on ice games and he is helping her in his research activities.

Meanwhile, Dorothy got the approval for her project from the Panel appointed by the President. They said this is something very essential that is why ancient sages may have advised kings to build places like Khajuraho and writing books like Kama Sutra. Family councils are good but cannot persuasive sufficiently on important and obscure matters which they can't orally described. They thanked Mrs. Senanayake for coming out with such a brilliant idea suitable for the country at this era.

Mrs. Senanayake who was in consultation with a Netherland company and they agreed to send the whole project in one week's time for approval and suggestion. These days she is fully involved in her project and could not go to the estate to help his friend Iqbal.

Iqbal informed a boat has arrived and go and clear it early otherwise they will go back.

She could not neglect Iqbal's request so he went to the estate with their driver.

On that day evening as there were not much of work in the bungalow and being a Saturday Minister has gone to a personal discussion with some of his political colleagues in Colombo. Sitha and Faizal were just chatting at the foyer. Nelly, their bionic dog was just listening to their gossips. Menika came and proposed Sitha to go for a walk with her child. Their dwarf, Juwa and other servant woman Josephine also was eager to accompany. Faizal said he has to take exercise and decided to stay back.

While they were walking along the Temple road when they were about less than a quarter mile away from the bungalow, a white mini-van came from behind, suddenly applied break and grabbed the child into the van and drive fast. All start crying and yelling. Sitha contact Faizal who came by the motor bike and got the information, rode very fast thinking that they may have gone towards the direction of Colombo. Mean while Sitha telephoned the police. They had the number of the van and the description. Police immediately rushed with the information, first went towards the Negambo beach as there were no clues, drive towards Colombo. Closer to Jaela from a distance they saw a white van knocked against a tree in the side of the road. When they come closer they noticed Faizal is wrestling with one guy, other one, the driver seems to be injured and unconscious. Child was crying on the ground. There were three police constables. One rushed to the spot and picked up the child and brought to the jeep. The wrestling guy was a robust fellow.

He was hand cuffed. Unconscious fellow was taken to the Jeep. Faizal said he will take the child to the bungalow and ordered them to take the injured fellow to the hospital. When regain consciousness to get a statement and if he is Okay, take both fellows into custody and lock up.

Police has battered the sturdy fellow well. He has referred to the driver and said he came on his instruction and did what he instructed to do. He is Mudliyar Relpanawa's driver.

Relpanawa is a good friend of Ursula's father, Kiriella, may be on his requirement to hurt the family of the Minister for a ragging instance in the university where his daughter Ursula was fallen from the upper floor and got her spinal cord affected.

Faizal knew the whole story and he did not encourage police to take further action. He thought this can be tackled in a different way. He telephoned affected girl's father.

"I heard you are a respectable thug in Balangoda. What made you to order that poor servant woman's child to be kidnapped."

"Who are you in the first place to inquire me something which I don't know."

"Don't be a coward Mr.Kiriella, I am Minister Religious Interests body guard. This servant woman and her child are living with us. So we have every right to look into these wretched affairs…"

"Now, Now now, what is the incident?" He inquired as he was not aware anything.

Faizal explained to him in short. But he denied totally. If the Driver of Relpanawa had given this order to his driver, it may be true, I'll agree. It is not an order given by me.

But just now I returned from Jaffna. He agreed to ask Relpanawa and thanked for enlightened him.

Mr.Kiriella, who is a member of the opposition group. He had asked several of his friends to teach some lessons to Senanayake's family as they are hiding Mangala.

Minister advised Faizal not to drag this affair as Mangala is no more in Sri Lanka.

"But if these sorts of things are happening I have to ask for a security unit to be stationed at the house, which I refused several times earlier."

As informed Dr. Guptha arrived to the Katunayake airport

on a Saturday early morning and Faizal picked him up and came over to the bungalow. When he was requested to have breakfast he responded that he had a shave, wash and breakfast in the flight now he needs a nap. He asked Sitha about the trip to Nuwara Eliya for which she answered that she will attend to it and requested father to have a nap for about one hour.

Sitha arranged everything on Mrs. Senanayake's advice and she requested Faizal to take the Benz as Doctor may be tired after coming all the way and he needs comfort. Faizal on his cell informed Kumari about their trip to Upasaka. She agreed to come early.

Faizal as usual accompanied, Kumari and along with Doctor and Sitha, left the place around eight and arrived Nuwara Eliya bungalow for lunch. They decided to go to meet Upasaka on the following day as Doctor was bit tired. A separate room was allocated to Dr. Guptha. As he is there Faizal also got into a separate room. However at night, Kumari came out and dragged Faizal into their room. Kumari laid in the centre. Sitha and Faizal in either side.

"Do you know why I dragged you over here. I got a fancy to have sex with you."

"Not today."Faizal said as Dr. Guptha is in the adjacent room.

"Why? Are you having period?" She put her leg over his legs. Sitha could not resist. She got up and entered the wash room. Waited there for nearly quarter of an hour and returned. She slowly crawled and covered with the cloth.

"Are you feeling so sleepy Sitha? We could not do anything with this guy."

"Sleep, sleep we have to leave early morning." Faizal ordered. "If that is an order, we will obey you Sir." Kumari crushed his hand and said.

Following day after breakfast they left the bungalow. On the way Dr. Guptha wanted to visit Sitha Amman Temple. They spent nearly half an hour. Doctor made a donation. They left to Katuwana. Had tea from a land -side kiosk. Arrived at Upasaka's hut around 11.30.

They all greeted Upasaka and came out and look around. Meanwhile Kumari approached Upasaka and asked whether the day is all right to receive the Mantra.

Upasaka said He was anticipating their arrival and prepared the Mantra for Kumari. It is in a talisman. He advised what obeisance she has to perform and remove the ola leaf and recite it 500 times per day. She thought it is a Herculean task but determined to do it. Around 12 after washing their faces and hands they went into the forest. Panther left the place when they were arriving. Upasaka went in and lit a coconut lamp, burnt the camphor and a bundle of joss sticks. He starts reciting Sthothra. Kumari dragged Faizal, came out and had a chat for about half an hour. Meanwhile Sitha and Doctor entered the tunnel and emerged in half an hour with respect and awe in their faces. When Faizal and Kumari entered, Upasaka got up, requested to leave without uttering anything unwanted. When they arrived at the hut a patient who has been stung by a cobra has been brought in. Upasaka had to attend to the patient. Others greeted him and left.

They returned to the Bungalow quietly had their lunch. All of them were very silent. Simon asked Doctor whether he needs a drink." No liquor, no liquor!"Doctor shouted. After the lunch they returned. He felt after coming from the den it is not congenial to consume alcohol.

While having dinner with the Minister and others Doctor said he had to go to India to perform a genitoplasty surgery to a pregnant woman whose husband and parents are known to him. When they questioned what it is he had to explain that most of the Indians have superstitious belief that the first child in a family should be a male. So this woman has confined with an embryo of a female child and it was seven months. So he said he has to change the sex. All were amazed and asked whether it is possible.

In India that surgery is common but legally not allowed. It conducts in private hospitals secretly. Charged 1.5 lakhs. But I did free.

Sitha asked why he did it free. Doctor said they are my friends and it was against my consciousness.

"This can have profound long term psychological effect on an individual, who might not accept the gender assigned by parents and doctors transform before age of consent. It is a highly sensitive issue from my point of view. Had I say no they would have developed a wrong opinion on me. So I agreed. I am reluctant to discuss on this. It is a secret!"

"I am also having a secret. A great secret." Mrs. Senanayake started.

"What is it Dorothy?" Doctor asked.

"For my project, my friend Iqbal agreed to spare me a 200 acre plot."

"That's great. Is it free?"

"Absolutely! But there are plenty of young coconut trees which have to fell down. If President comes to know, he will totally reject my project. So I have to keep my lips shut until he cuts down trees and donate me the bare land."

"Like our secret." Sitha ejaculated.

"Yes, Sitha" We have to obey Upasaka. Doctor said.

"I could not talk anything on my religious project with the Doctor. There is absolutely no secret involved. But it is for your information Doctor, 50% through."

"O, what a grand news!"

"When are you expecting to inaugurate it?"

"It will take time, it will take time. I'll invite you."

Their dinner was over. Doctor said he has to leave early and desired to go to bed straight away.

Following day, it was a Monday. Faizal dropped the Doctor at the airport and then after breakfast left with Sitha to the campus.

"How was the trip uncle? They didn't ask anything about me?" Mangala casually asked Dr. Guptha when he sat down for breakfast.

"Why not, I said you involved in my research activities and at the same time learning ice-skating, following a nursing course."

"My nursing course will start next month uncle. Now I am learning to dance on ice. Figure skating or what you called free dance."

"That is excellent!" Doctor said while flipping the News paper. Mrs. Guptha also joined with a glass of water in hand.

"Like aunty you also must drink a full glass of water in the morning."

"I had, of course. But I don't like to take too much of liquid in the morning. It is troublesome to go to the wash room often."

"I didn't want to ask you anything last night as you were exhausted." Mrs. Guptha said while drinking her water.

"Yes darling, I was terribly tired. I was not quite happy about the surgery although I performed it accurately."

"What was the surgery, uncle?"

"You are going to become a nurse. So you familiarize with these things. Genetoplastry."

"Oh! Sex transformation! Is it in Sri Lanka?""

"No child. In India."

"In Sri Lanka they do free for genuine cases. Doctors have discovered more than 500 female births with male organs. Their parents face social and psychological problems when they grow up. As such Lady Ridgeway Hospital for children in Colombo now undertake to do the surgery free of charge."

"In India also for genuine cases they do free. They called it esophageal replenish surgery. They have to pump with hormonal treatment as a part of the sex change procedure that may be irreversible."

"One of the nurses told me in Thailand this is something very common and it is a new culture. They do not want to perform surgery and change the sex. They grow like female and called in Thai, Katoey. They openly work in bars, hotels and night clubs."

"Yeah. Hermaphrodites!"

"She asked me to view them in the Internet. There are plenty, it seems."

"May be. In this area they are known as, Lady Boys or She males."

"What a world!" Mrs.Guptha exclaimed.

"So this couple is from Toronto, but still they haven't changed their attitudes after coming over to an advanced country like Canada. A Sikh couple."

"I am happy that I am a woman rather than a man."

"People should not go against the God." Mrs.Guptha uttered while applying butter on a slide of brown bread.

"Aunty, why do you eat brown bread. Your blood sugar level is not so high.No complaint about high cholesterol."

"No Mangala this is for uncle. I also prefer to go for brown. When you are becoming old you have to take all the precautions. Because,diabetes is the worst disease in the world."

"We have some more time. Anyway I am getting late." Immediately after breakfast she left.

"How was your trip to your Ramayana area?"

"Astonishing darling, astonishing! But Upasaka asked not to talk about anything what I witnessed in the cave. It was a big chamber, with full of brass ornaments. I saw the manuscripts of several books Ravana had written. It was in Brahmi or Nagari scripts, but I could not possibly read. To Sitha those were very clear.Sitha was able to peruse some, She enlightened me,she said Ravana was an astrologer who had an observatory to study the sky and he was a physician. She read the books of the names he had written.Manuscripts were there. She read the names. Kumara Thanthra,Nadi Pariksha,Uddisa Chikithsa,Herath Chikithsa,Vatika Prakarna and Rasarathnakaraya.Still I can remember them very well.However Upasaka advised not to talk about this. It is better not to divulge.Otherwise archaeologists will excavate and ruin the place.

But I am really happy darling. Really happy! It is because of Sitha I also was lucky enough to see all those archaic articles. Anyway don't tell anything to anybody. But believe Ramayana is a reality." Dr. Guptha also got up and went straight to computer room.

Rudolf telephoned the Doctor. "Doctor, good morning, I discovered something in my computer. It is amazing. I combined the reproduction of mental deliberation of a friend of mine in graphic technique. His romantic imagination was visible. Then I telephoned him and asked what he was doing. He said he was writing a letter to his fiancée. It was the same thing that appeared in graphic form on my computer screen."

"Possibility is there Rudolf. I am sure I could get what I exactly envisaged. We have to try again and again until we become successful."

"I'll come over uncle in the evening along with Mangala. Mangala is having a dance competition today.Figure Skating."

"Dance competition!" He thought for a moment,

"So early! Has she come to that level?"

"She is marvelous uncle. She picked up very quickly. Her body is very supple. She has the anxiety and the enthusiasm. I am quite sure she will master the subject very soon. She is desire to participate in winter Olympic with figure skating."

"That's great Rudolf. It is because of your enduring help. Keep it up Rudolf. Keep it up!"

"Thank you for your blessing uncle. Thank you. bye, bye."

"Bye."

He conveyed the current information to his beloved wife. She also was excited and extremely happy. He suggests that they should take her for a special feat.

"I got the first place in a dancing competition Aunty." Mangala immediately entering the condo with Rudolf was shouting from top of her voice with a huge smile. Mrs.Guptha hugged her.

Mangala was thrilled. The feeling of joy was exploding inside her when Mrs.Guptha embraced her like her own child. Thereafter all of them seated and was talking in high tone with laughing and gesticulations about all what she experienced and how she performed.

Mrs.Guptha suggests that they should celebrate and proposed to go to Hilton when Doctor comes. Meanwhile they had tea.

Mrs. Senanayake arrived in the evening from Iqbal's house

and informed over the telephone to her beloved husband that Iqbal has taken up her suggestion highly and agreed that he will get in touch with Brown and company where he has shares and proposed them to put up a tourist hotel. He will have a Cinema complex, with six halls and get a few fellows to have two or three restaurants, game centers, roller coasters, giant wheel with a carnival etc. it is going to be a massive entertainment complex. He also agreed to put up the building for my Khajuraho Art Gallery. I have no problems, however I thought I must establish a Council and a Fund to conduct the activities of my project and I thought Sitha to organize in collaboration with Chithrasena Dance Academy one or two dance shows to get funds for the project."

"Excellent Dorothy go ahead with all such activities keep inform the President. He will be delighted. I too have appointed a committee to look into everything relevant to my project.

With them I am going to Suriyawewa to look into the premises and make necessary arrangements. I have to make a helicopter trip. When I come home I will discuss all about the developments." Minister wound up the conversation.

On Mrs. Senanayake's suggestion Sitha had a chat with the Dance Academy. They were really delighted to conduct two shows at the BMICH and Lionel Wendt but with regard to a fund for Khajuraho Art Gallery project they desire to have a discussion with Mrs. Senanayake. Sitha conveyed this to Mrs. Senanayake their views. Mrs. Senanayake immediately initiated a call to Vajira and agreed to call over there for a chat.

In a month's time all arrangements were made with regard to the Dance recital. Sitha opted to perform, a Kandyan dance at the opening, one of her own creation and two of her western and Indian items.

Publicity campaign was given over to an Advertising Agency who agreed to do free of charge. Mrs. Senanayake herself made the payments for the two venues. It has been scheduled to stage on Saturday and Sunday.

First show was on Saturday at the BMICH.(fairly a big hall)The opening item was a New Kandyan Traditional dance created by Sitha Guptha. Introduction was given by popular Gunatunga Liyanage who is an announcer attached to Sri Lanka Broadcasting Corporation. At the outset he announced Sitha Guptha is a visiting lecturer at the Peradeniya University. She is a Canadian and an archaeologist by profession.

For the first 'welcome' item she has choreographed a modern Kandyan dance blended with Samba. Please welcome Sitha Guptha.

There was a thundering applause from the audience. Music was orchestrated mostly with Sri Lankan and western drums. Dance was very rhythmic and flawless. It was based on Thuranga Vannama.

Thereafter there were several items by Chithrasena Dance Academy. Sitha presented two more items. Media had covered the show and acclaimed very highly.

They had a big collection. Minus expenses the amount was Rs. One hundred thousand with which a Khajuraho Fund was set up. Presently almost all the work in the complex have started and likely to complete the entire set up very soon.

Tourist hotel is comprised with 50 rooms, Cinema complex with six halls for Sinhala, Tamil, Hindi and English movies. Three restaurants for Sinhala Indian and Western cusines. Roller Coaster, Giant wheel and other entertainments have been undertaken by a Canadian Company. Ferris wheel also has been proposed but as it is too tall and Airport is close by the idea has been dropped.

It is going to be a big complex with plenty of entertainments and Khajuraho is to be the main attraction with a knowledge enhancement purview.

"Dorothy" They normally have most of their discussions at the dinner time. It was a Friday night. Sitha and Faizal also sat down. "I had a thorough view at the land President has allocated. He has set apart 500 acres in case in the later stages we may require more spaces. Many new buildings are likely to come up. My secretary informed me there are three more countries have agreed to set up the replicas of famous religious places. At this rate some more will agreeable to my suggestions. We decided to name it as International Religious Complex."

"Are there any possibilities to earn some money?"

"No Dorothy, nothing at the moment."

"Chithrasena Academy is agreeable to organize two more Dance shows in Kandy and Galle. That will give further publicity to my project and it is an added advantage. With regard to fund raising objective they wanted me to come over there for a further chat. Sitha has got an appointment and I'll go there today. I can't possibly bother Iqbal for everything. I may have to suggest some other philanthropists to take the deal."

"Same advertising agency agreed to handle the advertising. Last time we gave them plenty of publicity. If Nawaloka owner was living, he would have helped us a lot.

"But his son is there. On the other hand you may get in touch with Maliban or Hotel Oberoi." Minister suggests.

"I'll telephone some of them tomorrow morning. Faizal can come with us?"

"Yeah, madam, after your discussion we can proceed to places you wanted until Sitha's class is over."

"Yes Faizal, but you never know what time our discussions will over and moreover doesn't know with whom we have to discuss. I may have to go with other guy, if the Minister has no other appointment." Dorothy lamented.

"At the moment nothing in my diary."

"That means you have to make some unwanted appointments?"

"No Dorothy, you can't expect a responsible minister to just stay at home."

"You need rest as you had a tiring trip today to Suriyawewa." Dorothy quips.

Why don't we recruit another driver. At least once in a way you must use your 180. What happened to the extra driver allocated earlier?"

"He is there in the office. He attends to my emergency trips."

"If need arises you can get down a driver with a vehicle from the Ministry Faizal suggests.

"Yes, there is no problem. Faizal is also there for emergency" Minister wound up. Nelly I want to go for a short walk. Will you accompany me." He asked Nelly who was squad down near them.

"Yes, walking is good for you. Walking keeps your blood vessels young."

"You are like a doctor."

"I am better than a doctor. Let's go." They stepped out.

"Coffee is ready madam." Menika brought on a tray. As minister was leaving, she went behind him and asked whether to bring his cup of coffee. Minister gave a negative reply. "I have a bit of constipation today. In any case keep it on my table in the room and cover with the dish." Minister took his walking stick and stepped out. A wall lizard cried.

"Bad omen Sir, better to stay for two minutes and leave."

"Is that's so. You too believe these superstitious things." Minister asked Nelly.

"Politicians take superstitions very seriously. Why not you?"

After two minutes they left. But didn't go very far. Returned in five minutes.

Faizal and Sitha came over to the foyer and sit down with cups of coffee in their hands.

"I have to go for a game of cricket, tomorrow afternoon. Do you like to accompany."

"all along?"

"Kumari will come."

"Then you don't want me."

"You can't do what she does."

"I am scared."

"Well. I don't want to ask." But he hold her palm and squeezed strongly.

"ui! Why do you want to hurt me."

"Because I love you."

"Yes, I know you guys have the liberty to marry four wives, for the variety sake. But how do you love several women at the same time."

"If you like to gain experience. You will realize."

" I can imagine. It won't be a true love."

"Love is blind."

"Blind people can make love better. Because anyone is same to a blind."

"Just like the fable where a blind recognized an elephant."

"First if he touches the head, O you are like a balloon my darling wife."

"Never know where he will touch next." They had a hearty laugh.

"You don't like to give me even a kiss." Faizal asked.

"I like but not here. Madam might see from a corner."

"Madam is busy with her project."

"What do you think about madam's project Faizal?"

"Exciting"

"Shall we go now?"

"Why, feeling sleepy."

"Yep"

"Then come to my room. Can have a hush hush talk."

"If Nelly sees she will complain to Madam."

"I don't think. I know about madam more than even her husband."

"I can guess."

"She is a nice woman. Very broad minded."

"Naturally. She is a philanthropist. Take from one side and gives from other side."

"Why, you don't like her."

"She is a mother to me. Now let's go. I'll practice half an hour what I have to dance tomorrow and then have a wash and come over."

"By that time I may be faster asleep."

"Then I'll turn back and go to my room. Or else you can have a romantic chat over the phone with Kumari."

"If I have a romantic chat with her, I don't know what will happen to you when you come."

"Let anything happen." She gave a pat on his butt and went to her room.

Following day, being Saturday, all the three, Mrs. Senanayake, Sitha and Faizal went over to Chithrasena Dance academy at Nawala. Vajira welcomed Mrs. Senanayake. They had a friendly chat and then she demonstrates about her Khajuraho program. Vajira got amazed, but gradually agreed with her concept. They agreed to contact several philanthropists who normally help them in their shows and requested Madam also to find some firms who could extend their cooperation. They had a chat for a few minutes and thanked Vajira for the assistance she extended for the earlier shows, and said she is going to ask the MPs at Kandy and Galle to undertake the full responsibility of the shows. Vajira responded "That is excellent. You may have to get a private bus for the transportation."

"She said. No problem. I'll get a luxury bus." At that time Sitha's dance class was over and they left. On the way Faizal said he has to go for a cricket session in the afternoon at the SSC.

"Sitha said she also like to witness the game."

"If you like you can come. No entrance fee."

"I don't mind you are going with Faizal but come home before mid- night. I have to be responsible to your Mama and Dada.

So that approval was quite sufficient for her. They left after lunch.

Kumari was waiting for them at the Pavilion.

Sitha went over and sat beside her. Two of her friends also arrived. Beula and Dulci.

"You didn't go for dancing today."Beula asked.

"Why not! Life itself is a dance."

"So you are dancing with the life?"

"Everyone does that."

"When is you engagement?" Dulci asked.

"Engagement on what?"

"On your marriage."

"O, my dear! I never knew you don't like me."

"I like you. That's why I asked."

"There is a heavy load in my head with several programmes. I have no time to think about getting a punishment for an imprisonment."

"You think marriage is an imprisonment?" Dulci questioned.

Match was started. "Kumari why are you silent?"

"Are you asking me to conduct a raid?"

"No child, express your opinion."

"I am a Police Officer. As Sitha said it would be an imprisonment. Police Officers have no free time to enjoy a married life. If you want to procreate children. Then could get married. Otherwise it is a taboo."

"What a disgusting life! Like a priest in a church or a monk in a temple, celebates. Faizal got a sixer. Brilliant one!" Beula shout.

"If somebody gets married and play brilliant shots. It's a merriment."

"Married life is not exactly like playing cricket. There are lots of ups and down. Another sixer!" Sitha exclaimed.

"Enjoy the cricket men, without talking rubbish." Kumari said while calling the snack boy and when he arrived got some potato chips and seven up bottles.

"Sitha tell me frankly why you think marriage is an imprisonment?" Dulci.

"It is Okay for those who want to become housemaid. Do cooking, look after the house and look after children, but for professionals there are other requirements in the prime of their lives. In my case I am almost a professional dancer, an archaeologist.

Do you think there will have spare time to lead a happy married life. It would be like a prison."

"Even in my case I am a police officer. 24 hours duty. No time to procreate children. If a man gets married to a person of my category, he will always go behind other women. It is Okay for you guys. Partrnership of Faizal and Sanath has come to 300. Oh, my gosh!'

"How brilliantly they play. But there aren't much crowd here." It was from Buela.

"Today there is a new movie at Regal. That must be the reason. Sitha shall we go for the 9.30 show?"

"No Kumari. Aunty wants me to come early. In addition to her Kahjuraho project she wants to have an Art Exhibition.

Incidentally day before night, she had given to wash all the brushes to a servant girl. It was after about 7.30 at night. So after washing she had thrown the water. Aunty has kept an Art board painted with white to dry. This woman has thrown those water from the bucket and accidently it has fallen over the Art board. In the morning aunty called me to show that. It was a beautiful allover pattern. This is the second time similar incident had happened.

I gave her an idea to draw a Kandyan dancing pose of mine over that. She must have done it. That's why she wanted me to come early to show it. Incidentally what is the movie?"

"Avatar."

"O, that's a long movie. Let's go tomorrow for 6.30 show."

"Ai, you guys won't see the game. Sanath out for no ball."

"Who is the next batsman?"

"I think Murali." Beulah uttered.

"Murali? What nonsense. Here comes Jayewardene." Kumari said and got up. "I'll go to the wash room and be back."She moved away.

"Hi, Sitha. Faizal is more closer to you or Kumari?"Buela asked.

"Naturally to Kumari."

"Or both are going to be his wives? Because he is a Muslim. The Cor'an allows to get married to four wives."

"And other two are going to be you two?"

"Nonsense! Our parents have selected partners for us."

"How on earth you guys know whether they are compatible to you?"

"Can't help. We have to adjust ourselves."

Kumari arrived. Got a call, "Sitha there is an urgent call for me from the IGP. I am leaving. Tell Faizal." She left in a hurry.

When the cricket match was over Faizal accompanied Sitha for dinner at Hilton and went back.

CHAPTER 6
Religious Complex – Figure Skating

Sunday is a busy day at the Minister's residence as they have to distribute 300 food parcels for destitute and other poor people. That is the great philanthropist activity of Mrs. Senanayake. Sitha also went over to the kitchen and help them to wrap food parcels. Faizal also came to help them. Meanwhile Sitha got a telephone call from her mama to say Mangala has got a fall from ski. .

"What! She is taking part in ski? How is the injury?

"Not severe. Sprain in the right leg. Any way admitted to the hospital. But she asked not to inform her mother. It is a minor thing."

"Mama I just can't believe that she has gone so far in a short time on ice sports."

"She is very clever."

They discuss several personal matters for a few minutes and wound up.

Juwa rushed to the kitchen and said. "There is a big crowd today, now itself.

Don't know, what is the reason?"

Menika went outside and had a peep. "What Juwa said is true. Is Ramazan today?"

"Today there is no Ramazan. O, today is a Thaipongal day. It may be the reason. You have to tell madam and increase the quantity." Faizal proposed.

"Menika go and tell madam." Proposed Bandara. Menika informed madam. She was reading the morning papers with the Minister. She immediately telephone two nearby hotels and requested to send 200 food parcels.

They started distribution at 12.While they were distributing, more and more people have arrived.200 parcels ordered also have brought. They distributed that too. But still was not sufficient. Minister got a bundle of 10 rupee notes and requested Faizal to go and distribute.

In the evening Mr. and Mrs. Senanayake with the driver cop went to Colombo to visit a friendly family.

Faizal Sitha and servant women with the child went to the Negambo beach.

"Sometimes back, Eric Leuthardt undertook the study with a team from the Centre for innovation in Neuroscience and Technology at the University of Washington to read someone's mind with the help of electrodes implanted in his head. But in my case I want to excavate what is in the mind without any electrode." Doctor briefed to Rudolf and Mangala at his computer room. Doctor further illustrates, "The mind is the nebulous thing that we associate with consciousness, feelings and thoughts. Brain is obviously connected to the mind and supports the mind's activity. Consciousness of the mind is the combined result of the electrical activity of the brain. Brain of a human being, say from about three years, can store, retain and recall information and experiences.

The faculty of retaining and remembering past experience and events can extract by quantum computer. Quantum computer is a new paradigm for physics with provocative implications in science and other areas of knowledge. The next major stage in the development of quantum theory is the development of the wave picture of matter and information. Computers have the ability to reproduce human voice. When sound reproduction is combined with the latest graphic technique we can get the information recorded in the cells of a brain. That is what we have to study and extract now." Doctor concluded.

"Apparently that won't be difficult if we employ nano-technology Doctor. When I go back I'll get experimented."

"Yes Rudolf make an attempt. However it won't be so easy. But you may have to try hard continuously.'

"I'll do it Doctor. Mangala also can help me."

Mangala has to go to the Nursing school. After she returns I'll engage."

"Thank you Rudolf."

They left.

"What is that you want to engage on when I return?"

"On the research."

"Oh I see."

"Don't become naughty."

"You are giving me ideas."

"Let the ideas develop."

"They are being developed."

They chat while driving. When it reached the Nursing Institute, Mangala gave him a passionate kiss and got down.

Mangala and Rudolf are now very close. Both of them developed a clear understanding each other. After the practical lessons in the Nursing Institute, Mangala went for ice hockey with Rudolf.

At the Women's Hockey Club at Toronto at that time there was not a big gathering, so until Mangala had a change Rudolf was engaged in a conversation with the Captain of the junior team.

"Your girl friend plays very well. We thought of making her the vice Captain of the team. But there is a rival, a Libyan girl. She is bit angry with Mangala. I observed it several times. She is a tuft character. Ask Mangala to be very careful."

"Thanks."

While the play was on Rudolf noticed several occasions that she tried to obstruct Mangala. In one occasion she pushed Mangala. She was thrown off and fallen down. In another occasion she put her leg between her legs and both were fallen down. Both of them had far too many physical contacts. Once instead of kicking the puck into the opponent's goal she purposely kicked it against Mangala's face. She came and battered her with her stick. She was fallen down. No punishment was given to her by the referee and this Libyan bitch was pretty wild.

When Mangala was in the dressing room, she came and pushed her. She was thrown off. But didn't return anything revengeful. She had a deadly frown. She removed all her costume including the knickers and got into a pair of jeans and a pull over without a bra.

After dressing up she came over to her car. Rudolf and Mangala went behind. Rudolf tapped at her shoulder with Mangala's stick.

"Hey what the dickens?"

"Why are you pushing this girl?"

"That's none of your business!"

"She is my girl friend. Next day if you harass her I'll put the puck in your mouth."

"It's game men it is a game. She has to face all these. Otherwise ask her to bugger off."

Mangala didn't want to involve. She was bit away from them. Then her boy friend arrived.

"What's the heck?"

"This bugger is trying to teach me how to play hockey."

"Are you asking for something?" He had a nasty look.

Then Mangala came and dragged him.

"If you want something stay here. Otherwise bugger off."

Mangala didn't want Rudolf to involve in and dragged him to the car.

Following day when Mangala was leaving Mrs.Guptha said "Don't involve in unwanted tussles. You never know these guys. They will do something to Rudolf. It is dangerous. These guys are always using revolvers. Our Government is not strict at all that civilians using firearms. Ask Rudolf to be away from them or you select some other place to play hockey." She advised.

"We are not cowards Mangala. Don't get afraid. Your Captain said Board wants to appoint you as the vice Captain. That's why the jealousy she is having."

On their way to working places they went for a snack to the nearby restaurant. There they met a Sri Lanka boy.

"I was a doctor in Sri Lanka. Came on a visit visa. Now the visa is over. They said if I am to practice here I must go to a varsity here and get qualified. Otherwise Sri Lanka degree is not recognized here."

"Yeah, to practice here you have to get qualified in Canada. You give up medicine and try to engage in some other field."

"My uncle is a doctor here. I can ask him whether there is any possibility."

"Absolutely nothing, Mangala. He can't do medicine here at the moment unless he earns a certificate from Canada. Best thing is to engage in some other field. But now you have a visa problem too. Anyway come and see me tomorrow at my office." He gave his visiting card.

Following day Rudolf was able to get a job in the motor mechanics garage where he used to get his car repaired. He warned, "Be careful as you don't have a visa."

In the evening when they went to Mangala's place Doctor had come early and was engaged in a conversation with Libyan Leader, Gaddafi. His picture was appeared in the Supercomputer. When they entered the computer room, while having the Conversation, doctor stretched his hand towards the screen of the Super computer for them to watch Gaddafi's bust. Rudolf eagerly looked at it. Conversation came to an end.

"I am successful to a greater extend Rudolf. Now I am encoding the picture. His views and response to my questions are satisfactory. He is likely to lose the battle. UN is not giving any support to small countries. See what happened to Iraq! In mid 2002 the US began to explore the option of invading and dislodging Iraqi President Sadam Hussain. After a trial he was killed like a pauper. Accusation was that he has produced chemical weapons. Kofi Anan and several experts entered there for a careful investigation. But there was absolutely no such weapons. Subsequently on Hosni Mubarak of Egypt, Colonel Gaddafi in Libya, all were accused on corruptions. Which they cannot prove and it is a vague term. But these Leaders will be killed and the countries would be ruined. However, I couldn't get the picture with lips sinks while Gaddafi was talking to me. I must try to get that too. Then my research is half way completed."

Doctor was extremely happy.

"Yes Doctor. What other information you exactly expected to achieve?"

"I wanted to get a person's future plans on any subject and

whether he will have any response if I question him on what he is at the moment thinking on. That information is bit difficult to signify. But I'll try my level best and tackle all these."Doctor was adamant.

"You will be successful Doctor, I am quite confident."

"You know relevant to Gaddafi, Super Powers in the world, America and NATO countries, they jealous of other small countries are coming up. They always try to crush. They get round a few fellows who are against governments, give them high hope and incited them to go against the lawfully established Governments. They have half way ruined Libya. Killed so many innocent citizens. Why on earth they have such a jealousy towards other small countries.

What business they have got to involve. I completely agreeable with Gaddafi. America has no business to involve and get NATO to ruin that country."

"Exactly…Mangala too involved in a Libyan tussle yesterday."

"Yeah. I heard, but don't involve because ordinary citizens are also must be in bad mood. So whenever there is a bit of an involvement, they too like to hang on. Do avoid."

"Yeah. We don't want to. Mangala is likely to be appointed as the Vice Captain. So that girl has a jealousy over it."

"Such tussles always exist in teams. You can't avoid. But better to be away from involving in fighting. Results perhaps would be unexpected."

"Yeah uncle. Mangala agreed."

Following day they came with the good news to confirm Mangala was appointed as the Vice Captain of the team.

So they decided to celebrate by visiting CN Tower for dinner.

They sat on a table in the revolving area. On that particular day CN Tower was lit with bright yellow in respect of the funeral of the Leader of the Opposition. Jack Layton. Very energetic politician. Worked very hard during the election and gained the next highest number of winning members. He agreed to work with the Prime Minister cordially. But he develops cancer and within one month died."

"He will go to heaven."Mrs.Guptha quips. When waiter brought the dishes that she ordered. Mangala said,

"I don't think they have luxury food like this in the heaven."

"No food is necessary for them. They survive without food or drink or whatever. That's why you called it heaven. If they think something they will get it immediately and just fulfilled without consuming."

"Mangala do you know this tower was the highest in the world few months back?"

"Is that so, uncle?"

"Now, Burj Khalifa in Dubai." Rudolf intervened.

"Yeah! Now Saudi Arabia wanted to give a competition. They wanted to build a tower higher than that.Crazy!' Dr.uttered.

Mrs. Guptha wanted to know something about Rudolf and she asked, "Rudolf. How old are your parents."

"My parents are not living aunty. My grandfather was involved in the war. He has been branded as a Nazi criminal. There was a trial against Nazi criminals in Nuremburg. While the trial was going on he died in the court. After his death my parents have migrated to America and they were in California. There had been a bush fire and our house also got blazed. We were rescued by a party who were living close by. Parents got charred and we didn't get the opportunity to have a glance at them."

"You don't have any brothers or sisters?" Doctor asked.

"I had a brother. But I don't know where he is. Both of us came over to Canada together to study. He wants to become a doctor and joined a University in Vancouver and I came to

Toronto and joined the branch of IBM. Left couple of years back and joined the present company."

They talked about their personal affairs for a short while. Then a young man passed their –place twice looking strongly at Rudolf.

"Don't look at him Rudolf; he is the person who challenged Rudolf for a fight." Mangala hushed.
Mrs.Guptha. "Don't involve in."
Then he came closer and addressed, "Rudolf!"
Rudolf looks at his face for two seconds. Got up suddenly and embraced him.
Then Rudolf introduced, "He is my brother, Carl Jung." He stretched his finger towards Dr. Guptha and said He is Dr. Indrajith Guptha, a Gynecologist, and Mrs.Guptha. And then to Mangala, She is…"
"Your girl friend…"Jung completed.
"…Mangala" Then he turned to Jung and said "I'll come after the dinner. Give me five minutes."
"Then I'll wait downstairs."
"Okay."
He left.

"What a coincidence! It is after about 15 years."Amazed Rudolf.
"However meeting him just at a time we were talking about him is a surprise."Doctor said.
Rudolf finished his food hurriedly. "I'll go and talk to him and be back, Bye!" He left.
"It is a real coincidence!" Mangala exclaimed.
"I don't think there will have any more fights. Nothing to worry!" Mrs.Guptha had no suspicion.
In a few minute they left talking about Rudolf's reunion.

CHAPTER 7
Khajuraho – Dorothy's deception

Khajuraho Art Complex has been inaugurated and it is in full swing now. Mr.Iqbal is taking ample interest over the entire area including the tourist hotel.Government is getting an additional revenue from this complex for each and every entertainment owner have to obtain a licence.Iqbal evinces a greater interest on this rather than the drug business. Mrs. Senanayake asked him to give up the drug transaction that she is also like to keep away altogether. By any chance if it busts up our whole reputation will go to dogs. Iqbal said he has realized it and already had sent the final letter to Thailand dealer. This is last consignment. It is fairly a big one and gets it cleared carefully.

It was a Friday. Faizal has gone with Sitha to the Campus, as she has been scheduled to deliver a talk on archaeology in Canada, for those who are engaged in archaeology and others on allied subject. Minister has gone to Suriyaweva to see the position of the construction of several religious replicas and will not avail for two days as President like to be with him. Mrs. Senanayake has revealed that she has been invited some of her friends who have agreed to come and pick her up. She is too likely to be away for two or three days.

She thought she must go in disguise as her job seems to be bit bigger than earlier assignments. She got ready like a house maid with chintz and a jacket without any jewellery. She got down a taxi and left requesting Nelly and Menika to look after the house for one or two days as she is likely to be out.

When she arrived at the house at the estate like a house maid in a taxi, Joseph Appuhamy, the person who look after the estate got amazed but didn't ask anything. He knows about her drug dealing but nobody else. I have no time to waste Joseph. I must get the stuff and leave soon either by the bus or a Taxi. By that time Joseph already collected the stuff, fairly a big lot and it was in a suit case. He asks Joseph to take the suit case and accompany her to the road. When they came to the road she asked him to go back and she will get the bus. He was reluctant to keep her all along, however can't possibly ignore her order. He turns back and entered the land but was hiding behind a tree until she leaves. She raised her hand and stopped a taxi that was riding towards Negambo and talked to the driver and discussed. Then Joseph returned.

Driver has told he has come to drop a friend and he is not the owner of the taxi. Now he is going to Colombo can give a lift. She can offer a reasonable amount.

"Then you can give a lift free of charge."

"Well there is a risk. To cover up you may pay something reasonable. As you are planning to go abroad for a job, you must be having money."

"I'll pay you 400/-"

"Okay madam, hop in."

On the way he has told he has a property close by where he has to go and be there for couple of minutes to collect a few young coconuts. He is planning to sell that as it is troublesome to come all the way. She has not made any comment but has told that she has to go to the Job Agency without delay.

Taxi turned to an estate and had to go bit interior to the house. An elderly man came out.

He ordered him to get some young coconuts for him to take home and to cut one for this lady. She said "No" but he ignored as he didn't hear that and went in. She thought if she is selling the property and if it is reasonable she can have a deal. She covered the suit case with her neck shawl and got down. Young coconut was cut for her and he called her. She went in. Without the shawl her plumed breast was eye catching. As she was looking at the house, he just make a hint to her when you return from the foreign job, with lot of money, you can by this. It is very cheap. Five lakhs only. She was interested to look into the rooms and went in further. This is with attached bath room. Other one is much better. The master bed room. She went to the next where there was a bed also. He tries to accost her. But she repelled. Then he holds her tight and tried to kiss her. She bit his lip. Then he gave a thundering slap at her face. Her lip was burst. He tied her both hands from behind to the bed. She started yelling and bent down to remove her sandal to hit him. Then some money and cell phone dropped down. He quickly picked both. Lock the door. He told the man "Don't open the door. I'll buy a bottle of arrack and some curries to have lunch. You prepare some rice and a sambol."

Earlier also he has brought women and has paid him satisfactorily. On the way he checked her suit case to find whether there is any valuable. He got amazed when he opened up the suit case. It was full of drugs. He changed his idea. He decided to drive direct to Colombo. On the way he hid the suitcase inside the boot and covered up with some junks that were in the boot. Informed Wennappuwa Police over the cell.

"Inspector, when I am coming from Puttalam, an innocent woman was on the road who wanted to go to Negambo and asked for a lift. I offered. She was a mad woman. Hit at my head and started harassing me and was scolding in filth. I dropped her at a house at number 200. About half a mile away from your Police station. Put her into a room and locked up. There is a man. I told him that I'll inform the police. Please go and remove her and take her to Angoda. That man is scared. My name is Rupasinghe. My car number is 10 Sri 9000. I think DIG knows me. I'll inform him too."He gave a bogus name and a wrong car number.

As he said he knows DIG and he will inform him too. Police immediately had gone there. At that time she has made a mess and was behaving exactly as a furious mad woman. She had to adopt that attitude purposely to cover up herself, Minister and Iqbal from everything. They have taken her to the Wennappuwa Police Station and locked up. O/IC had gone to Colombo for a private party. Officers did not want to telephone but decided to keep her until he returns to find what steps should be taken.Till midnight he did not return. This woman was very boisterous and pouring blood from her mouth. They could not take her to a doctor. Then thought of taking her to the Mental Asylum as informant directed.

Mrs. Senanayake did not return for two days. Then they started telephoning several known places. When they telephoned their estate, the man said she returned by a taxi. Minister ordered Faizal to inform all the Police stations. When the Wennappuwa Police Station got the radio message, they never suspect the victim they admitted to Mental Hospital could be Minister's wife. So they did not make any response.

Minister did not want to publish in any news papers or

inform the media. He had a suspicion on the man whose daughter got spinal cord injury may have done something to revenge. From all the other sources they tried their level best to trace her. Everything were futile. Bungalow was like a funeral house. Iqbal suspects something may have happened because of the drug transaction. But scared to come out with anything.

There was a news item to say a young woman has been killed and dumped in a jungle plot near Puttalam. They suspected that could be of Mrs. Senanayake.They went to the spot with bionic Nelly and a Police Unit. Bionic Nelly could not identify. She didn't sniff even. It was almost decomposed and apparently animals have consumed the head and hands. But was looked like that of Mrs. Senanayake as there was a gold ring quite similar to what she normally used to wear. The body was brought to the mortuary.

Minister was quite confident it could be his wife. "It is no doubt, my wife. Let us make arrangement to take the body home. Faizal."

Nelly murmured "How can this man identify her body he may not have even touched her body recently."

"Faizal like a good boy attend to all what are necessary. Let us have a cremation. Although she was Minister's wife, they had the funeral in a low scale as they were reluctant to publicize for some reason or other.

When Doctor Guptha got the pathetic news immediately made arrangement to travel to Sri Lanka with the wife and Mangala.

After the funeral was over Faizal said that he does not like to stay any longer in the bungalow but he likes to get married to Sitha. Sitha was agreeable but said must wait for some times.

Sitha's parents also had no objections. But they too advised that it is better to wait for sometimes.

Faizal dialed Kumari who was about to sleep and questioning why she is sleeping early and her response was not that satisfactory, may be perhaps he did not go to meet her or talk to her whole day however, quite openly he said, "Kumari, I have decided to marry Sitha. One day you too will take a decision like this. That would be the day that you will let somebody love you the way you deserved to be loved."

She didn't utter a word but her eyes were swinging in tears. Her lower lip was quivering like fluttering of a banana leaf due to speedy wind. She felt she is burning with a rousing anger. Her eyes glittering with moisture of tears. "If you desired why should I raise any objection. Remember the first day! I haven't still forgotten it. Don't totally knock me off." She was desperate.

"No Kumari, I'll be with you. Our friendship will remain as it was. I arrive at this decision as I felt after the death of Mrs. Senanayake ,we are all in a labyrinth. Sitha too felt the same. So to avoid the chaos we arrived at this decision. I'll visit you tomorrow morning to have a chat, before you are going to the office. Bye!"

She did not respond but Faizal kept the receiver.

Following day early morning he got up and got ready but Minister summoned and requested to accompany him to Suriyaweva.

Dr. and Mrs.Guptha with Mangala who came for the

funeral without making much arrangement at their ends wanted to return in a hurry. But Mangala's mother, Mrs. Mahawalathenna who had come for the funeral wanted them to visit their place and Mangala was desired to pay a visit to Ursula. So all of them made a trip to Balangoda. It was 96 miles from Temple Road, Negambo.

Immediately they went over Mangala suggests that she wanted to visit Ursula with the Doctor. She telephoned to find whether they have any objection. They were anxious her to visit and Ursula's mother said that they have no grudge at all. She repeatedly said she never pushed her but wanted to prevent her. She responded that they have realized it and asked her to visit. So she went over with the doctor along with a valuable present from Canada.

Doctor who examined Ursula felt that her spinal cord injury could be cured. He said endoscopic laser spine surgery is available in Canada. However he said he must get a few x-ray pictures and a biopsy from a nearby hospital. She was taken to Balangoda hospital and on doctor's request several x-ray pictures and a biopsy were taken. Ursula's mother said to the doctor. "This is a great favor Doctor, if you can do something. I am prepared to pay any amount as this is an agony to a young girl like Ursula. Due to sheer ignorance of the University authorities they had allowed young boys and girls to involve in wretched ragging."

Doctor said when he go back to Canada check with his orthopedic surgeon and inform them what should be done. If it has to be done in Canada, patient has to be taken over there. For that Ursula's mother agreed. Ursula and her mother were extremely happy and said they will be eagerly waiting to hear from them soon. Mangala gave a long hug to Ursula and left with the Doctor.

They had early dinner at Mangala's house and returned before mid-night. Following day morning they arrived at the Katunayake Airport and returned to Canada.

Sitha did not want go with her parents but decided to stay as she has to attend to the Peradeniya University as a lecturer and also as Minister would be all along if she leaves. She wanted to attend to all the work at the bungalow as well as to help the minister in every possible way. She also wanted to look into the affairs of the Khajuraho project which Mrs. Senanayake launched.

When doctor returns had a thorough check and found nothing had happened to the spinal cord according to the x- ray pictures, some discs had been cracked and do not act as cushions between spinal vertebrate. The outer wall of the discs which are made up of cartilage while the centre is jelly like.

They have been maladjusted but could be replaced with artificial discs according to orthopedic surgeon and it could be totally cured by laser surgery. Doctor informed Mrs. Mahawalathenna and agreed to send a suitable letter for enable them to obtain visas.

Faizal decided to resign from the Police Service after they fixed their marriage. Minister decided to appoint him as the Secretary once he resigned from the Police force. Minister further said as he has no children he will treat Sitha and Faizal as his own children and willing to entrust all his properties to them. So that they need not go anywhere else but could remain in his house. He will officially transfer everything's to their names. Well in advance he said he will fix a date for the marriage immediately he officially and ceremoniously opened up the Religious Complex, which is likely to take about six months.

With regard to Ursula's treatment, she went over to Canada with her mother.

Ursula was admitted to the Orthopedic Clinic and mother was allowed to stay with Dr and Mrs.Guptha.

Mangala was still feeling sorry and pleaded Ursula's mother not to have any hard feeling that she never pushed her.

"We have realized that later and I have faith on you child. Why on earth, University authorities allow these young boys and girls to have animal pleasure by allowing them to conduct wretched ragging? That is what I can't understand." She was lamenting.

"It was a carnal pride to them aunty moreover it has become a tradition. They must not go that far to make young girls naked in front of young boys. Females have the shame unlike boys. For fancy sake if they conduct decent fun is all right. But they must not go to the extent of removing girls clothing up to the nudity. That's inhuman."

"I must ask your Religious Minister to take this up in the Parliament and totally ban it. University youths must pay full attention on their studies."

"Minister Uncle is a very neutral person. He will present it in a mediocre poise. Let's request him to do so. If it has happened in Canada perhaps could sue the University Authorities."

"It should be."

After two months Ursula became quite well and was able to walk. They returned .The disunity exists between the two families was completely diminished. Faizal attempted to find out whether Ursula's father has some involvement with regard to the death of the madam. He made investigation secretly and quietly. He knew the grudge they had with the

Senanayake family earlier in the assumption that they were hiding Mangala.

The two Dance Recitals arranged when Mrs. Sennayake was living have to be performed as tickets have been sold and publicity has been extensively carried out. However Sitha has no burden as Vajira has taken the entire responsibility. Sitha has to present her items only. Faizal agreed to accompany her.

CHAPTER 8
Heaven and Honour killing

---◇---

"Hi, a new lady! From where on earth you came over here?"

"I am living in a branch of heaven in Sri Lanka. But it has now gone to dogs. So I skipped over here before my death. Can I be here for one hour?"

"A branch of heaven! And you came before your death?"

"Yep. Some police officers dumped me there and said this is a heaven. I entered and went interior. It was not a heaven. It was worse than a hell. An attendant came and gave me a robe. I got into it and left my clothing in a locket. Attendant said this the dinner time. If you are not after the dinner you may go to the dining hall and have something. I had little hunger. So I went over there. At that time two young damsels were fighting each other. Fighting with their plates. One had got a cut. Other one had curry and rice all over her body. No one comes forward to settle their dispute. I just couldn't look at these innocent young girls are fighting each other. I approached.

"Who are you?"

"I am a minister's wife."

One worships me. I asked "Why are you fighting?"

"This woman has eloped with my husband. I was searching for her all over. Only now I met her…"

"He was not anybody's husband men. He was a University boy. He was bordered in our house. I got friendly with him. We were waiting until his final exam is over to get married. Meanwhile there was a strike in the University claiming for more facilities for them. I knew they will never get what they are agitating for. I suggest him to elope."

"He is not my husband darling?"

"No men."

"I am so sorry darling. Go and get somebody else's plate and eat." She kissed her on her head and wanted to go and wash her body as there was so much of curry on her breast. Then she turned to me and asked,

"You came for dinner, being a wife of a minister! Just smell curry on my body. Stinky, like stale food. Can you eat these things? Go back to Hilton and have some barbecue.bye!" she got vanished.

"I heard you are a wife of a minister." Another middle age one approached her.

"Why did you come to this dungeon? Can you eat this rubbish in the lunatic asylum? I'll get some high class food from our attendant's room. They used to rob all good stuff from here leaving us the rubbish. Wait a minute."

She left and came in a minute with the garbage bin.

"See madam! They have eaten all the good stuff. Even what they have dumped in to the garbage can is better than what we eat. Take some from this."

"No thanks."

"You are a damn proud woman. You know where you are now? You are in a lunatic asylum. Your ministers have a canteen in the Parliament, where food is excellent but very cheap. What is worth fifty dollars, you guys get for one dollar. Here in the lunatic asylum getting something of that level is like finding a needle in a haystack. You proud woman, bugger off from here men! Leave this place for us to enjoy. Take this garbage bin and vanish."Ha, ha, ha! She had a mockery laugh. Then an attendant came over and pulled her and dragged to the room. I couldn't stay there any longer. I came and slept with a heavy head. I don't know how I have tossed over here."

"Oh I see. You are very lucky to tossed over here. This is the heaven. What is your name?"

"I am Dorothy, wife of the Minister for Religious Interests of the Government."

"Being a wife of a Minister you came to heaven. Very strange! This is a rare opportunity for a wife of a politician to ascend to heaven. Now Dorothy this is the only heaven in the Universe. Only those who have committed some extraordinary good work get the opportunity to ascend here. Our rules and conditions are very much different from human world. In the first place you must throw away what you are covering your beautiful body. Don't hesitate."

"O, I feel shame madam. Grown up never does that in our world in an open place like this?"

"Heaven is an open place. There are no secret cubicles. All are with open minds. You can't hide anything here. That's why you can't hide your body with cloth or any other material. You must be in clean nude. Open minded. Nothing to hide. Nothing to worry." She sat down on a beautiful ceramic chair.

"There are no males here. Why on earth you should feel ashamed. You guys in human world always hiding things. Your body is a plain truth. You must not hide the truth. Politicians always do that. Naturally you also may have that influence. Please don't hide your beautiful body Dorothy. Truth is there in the body. Body is the truth. If you see the nude body often, there is nothing unusual. You won't be born with cloth. That is not the nature. Never go against the nature. Sit now."

"Excuse me madam! Could I go to the bath room and be back?"

"Ha,ha,ha, she laughed and said there are no bath rooms in the heaven."

"Is that so? Doesn't matter. When I go back to the Earth I can go."

"Pardon me Dorothy!" She tendered her apology for the short coming and explained it not quite necessary for the haven."

Oh! It is very strange. She said to herself.

"Dorothy, I was a beautiful talented movie personality in human world. I did lot of bad things as my male counterparts forced me to do. Now no more harassment. Fortunately no more males here, except our old King. He won't get down from the thrown. So we have no fear or suspicion. We need not bother about him.

I am confident what all I did were good things. Otherwise you can't expect me to come over to this beautiful place called by religious leaders as heaven. My name was and is Marilyn Monroe. You may address me as Marilyn. I came here on August 5th 1962, immediately after my painful death. Taking into consideration the excellent bit of work that I performed to keep the human beings in happy mood, I got the opportunity to ascend to this sphere. This place is meant for only good, honest people. Here comes a friend of ours. Meet Diana." She introduced her. "She is Dorothy. A wife of a Minister in Sri Lanka."

Diana extends her hand. "How do you do!"

"I am fine. Very glad to meet a person like you Diana."

"She is a lady who has done lot of good things when she was in human world. Ultimately she got a divorce from the Royal prince, and met with a nasty accident in Paris, while driving the car in a terrific speed. So she got the opportunity to come over here. She how beautiful she is without clothing. She is clean, neat and hiding is not the practice here. She is having open mind too without any secret. There is no alternative Dorothy. You have to cast away your filthy cloth."

She removed the robe.

"Although Marilyn used the term filthy it is not in our heavenly Oxford dictionary Dorothy. Our dictionary is very thin. All the bad words have been removed."

"Yeas Dorothy. What Diana said is perfectly correct. No bad, foul words in it." Marilyn ascertained.

"How did you come over here, being a wife of a politician, Dorothy? Even rarely do they perform anything good, people never recognized what they have performed is something good. Because often they will charge with corruptions. Whether those are true or false. " Diana sat on a comfortable chair and Dorothy questioned her with a thousand watt smile.

"Amidst bad things I also may have done a bit of a good work which enables me to ascend to the heaven. However Diana as there are no males here you are safe. Otherwise a nude body like yours is sufficient for men to get mad."

"If they are mad they can't come here."

"I was mad but I came here. I was an inmate of the Mental Hospital in Sri Lanka was admitted on a full-moon day. So my brain got afflicted due to lunar effect. For some valid reason concerning me I had to get adopted artificial lunacy. That generates an unexpected chance to come here before the death."

Diana had a –that can't be-type of a look.

"Well Diana. I was a philanthropist. But of course I have to be franked I was up to plenty of mischief also. Otherwise you can't be a philanthropist in a country like Sri Lanka. Towards the end I had the luck to engage in a very praiseworthy undertaking. An extremely beneficial bit of work for married people. I fully satisfied with it. It is definitely a meritorious act. That's why perhaps, I was able to come over here prior to my death."

"What was it Dorothy? Marilyn asked.

"I opened up a Khajuraho in Sri Lanka."

"What on earth is Khajuraho?" Diana was inquisitive.

"Kahjuraho is in India. It has built up in an area of 20sq kilometer in the Madhya Pradesh in the 10th century. There were 8 gates and 80 temples. Now there are only 25. A vast place. The place is with full of erotic sculptures based on a very valuable book by Vathsallya's, known as Kama Suthra. It was a very analytical book on sexology written for human souls to have happy married lives. You know marriage was created for the well being and happiness of mankind. Man has realized the difficulty, trial and tribulation, he has to undergo once get into a wed lock. Problems will crop up one after the other. Only remedy is sexuality. Sexuality is an innate nature of human beings. They can forget their all the burdens and achieve a comfortable position if they know the art of sex on the golden advises of sages, kings who have fully understood the value of it built a vast museum with religious shrines. When it's interwoven with religion people have enormous faith to believe what they have displayed. When I visited this place, realized why they have taken such a pain and spending colossal amount of money and built this. So I decided to have a replica in my country. After so many discussions with authorities and legal personalities I built it with the help of one of my cordial Muslim friends. It is an Art Gallery. All sexual pictures in video clips are exhibiting to married people and others over 18 who are to be married. It is a horse shoe like building, where there are two rows one for females and one for males. They can't see each other. Demonstrations on video clips starting from the stage of onset of puberty. It goes up to their death at the old age with ample techniques on sexology. I*n between there are* short lectures on HIV, gonorrhea, syphilis etc for them to take precaution in their life and then condoms, rejuvenating drugs for erectile dysfunction etc. with all necessary instructions available to them to have a happy life without any disability."

"It is an excellent job! Excellent job Dorothy. If I was in Sri Lanka I would have gone to watch your excellent project with my Prince. Then I would not have a divorce."

" Anyway during that time I haven't seen even Khajuraho."

"Yeah, I had my divorce on 28th Aug.1996, one year prior to my death. I was very unhappy and dreary. May be because of that I had a car accident and occurred my death."

"Anyway now you are extremely happy Diana here in the heaven."

Marilyn said.

"Happiness is something very essential for any person to lead an excellent life. The aim of my project is also exactly the same. To achieve happiness is the prime aim."

"Aren't you happy Dorothy now? After coming over here for this few minutes you have changed and had become beautiful. You have become radiant. Your face also somewhat changed. In heaven you don't required L'Oreal, Lancôme, Dior, Elizabeth Arden etc. to become beautiful. Keep your skin and hair much smoother than silk. Beauty and the shape gradually will encompass your body. In another few hours time you will be like Venus. Wait and see." Marilyn was joyful.

"May be but I am anxious to help people in my country. I am a philanthropist."

"There is a very deep philosophy in your whole project." Diana said. "I was more worried about millions who were suffering due to poverty in certain countries. Children had no food no clothing. No medications they were living miserably. Living like dead bodies. I engaged in helping them with genuine charity work. That's how I came to heaven."

"Do you know your eldest son, William got married."

"No! These boys are very ungrateful. Never inform me."

"Don't blame them Diana. How do they know you are here. We don't have media to publicize anything in the heaven." Marilyn said.

"To whom he got married Dorothy?"

"To one Kate Middleton. A cute beautiful lady. A commoner"

"That's Okay. That's perfectly all right. There is no law that they must get married to one with Royal blood. Those are outdated concepts."

"I don't think William will follow his father."

"You can't blame the Prince Dorothy. If your Khajuraho was there in London, perhaps this may not have happened. Human weaknesses are there. But now he is married to another lady. He must be happy. I pray him. Even in Royal families these things happen. You can't avoid." Diana was in bit penitence.

"For their wedding procession there was a huge crowd. Procession was from Buckingham Palace to Westminster Abbey. Now they are being addressed as the Duke and Duchess of Cambridge.'

"I have absolutely no interest in those pseudo titles. Ordinary people don't like Royal people now. You know what happened to Sadam Hussain, Hosni Mubarak, and Muammar Gaddafi. What a colossal amount of money our Royal family in London is devastating. All are rate payers' money. They must not live majestically with rate payers' money. There are millions suffering without food, shelter, medications. They must realize these situations and give their kingships and should live like ordinary people without gormandizing wealth. All monarchies, dictatorships should disband and give its place to democracy in this 21st century. Democracy also should never ever sustain as a lunacy." Diana lectured them.

"Now who is the king in the heaven? Still Sakkara?" Dorothy asked.

"Oh, no! That man dead and gone to hell! He did lot of mischief things when he was here. All the ladies got together and kicked him at the butt and pushed him down. Now one Dharmasoka from India is here. He is very feeble but a righteous King. He is always on the thrown. Never ever looks at girls." Marilyn responded as the Supervisor in the heaven.

"Oh my God! That Dharmasoka. He was known as Chandasoka. He killed millions of people. How on earth he became a king in the heaven?"

"To compensate all his crimes he has done lot of charity works at the end. That helped him to come over here as a king. But not as an Emperor. Any way in the heaven he can't mix up with us. We are being females superior here. That superiority is never recognized on the Earth. See, every king, every dictator, every leader, and every man even a sage is alive on Earth, because a mother gave birth. A mother, woman opened to suffering. Human leaders or anyone still this truth is not recognized. The truth is not respected. The truth is not honored. Instead of being recognized for birthing. Instead of being respected for birthing they are being raped. They are abusing and beating for no reason. They are being murdered. Hope your Khajuraho enlightens them with some sense. Here comes a young one. How on earth you came here in this tender age and from where?" Marilyn questioned when a young approached them.

"My brother and father strangled me to death and I am from that vast, rich and modern country, Canada."

"Father and brother! They didn't like you."

"They were living in primitive culture with obsolete ideas although they migrated to Canada. They live according to the outdated principles of the Mosque. They desire us to live like in desert. Where there is scorching sun and sands storms.

They ordered us to cover our heads with a head gear, called Hijab. I was involved in volunteer and lots of social work in addition to my university activities. With such duties it is very uncomfortable to wear a Hijab in a country like CANADA. So I gave it up. My ignorant father and brother who were hanging on to the desert culture forced me to wear Hijab, a piece of cloth to cover the head. I am from an advanced town called Mississauga. My name is Hervaz. I am a student of Toronto University. Several days they scolded and threatened me. One day when my mother was not at home, I was strangled brutally. It was a murder committed in the name of a twisted sense of family honour. Sheer madness! They have named it as 'honour killing.' In India, in certain areas cell phones have been banned. It seems young boys and girls talk over the phones and elope. When they come to know where they are they will cut the neck and kill her. Police do not interfere. No case nothing. Justice has nothing to do. Contemporary tales of massacres erupting in certain villages where they follow age old customs. A marriage is sanctioned if it satisfies age-old customs. If anybody defies their rituals, an unofficial death sentence is passed and executed in the most gruesome way. But some defy these age-old meaningless customs connected to their religious rituals and bold enough to take steps in their own way and leave the village and go to a remote area. My case is something even relatives of ours in Canada do not approve.

It goes as a high-profile murder case in Canada generated international attention and continued to be the subject of worldwide interest. My involvement in volunteer work on non-Muslim teenage activities provoked my father and brother due to sheer ignorance because of the religion and culture. It's a menace! I feel sorry about them.

They still believe we should live like in a desert although we have come to an advanced country like Canada.

In India marrying outside one's caste is a common reason for honour killing. Again in India girl child is considered a burden and do not hesitate to kill the female foetus inside the womb. Orthodox cultures across South Asia honour killing has become a common malady. When they occur in Canada, one is forced to ponder on how deeply entrenched these outdated value systems are, which they can't do away with. According to United Nations Population Fund, around 5000 women annually murdered in the name of honour killings.The source of these practices can be traced in deeplyrooted social prejudics prevail in orthodox cultures, in India,Pakistan and such regions."

"My dear Hervaz I am sorry about the backwardness of your father and brother and no love to their own blood.These outdated abominable cultures not fitting at all to the 21 st century.It is the responsibility of respective governments that should completely ban them from the society. Why aren't they open their eyes and take remedial measures.

Make your complaint to the King. He will give them a rigid punishment without any mercy and Let the God teach other ignorant people to take your case as an example. I'll come with you." Marilyn suggests "let's go the righteous king." Marilyn accompanied her and when she was returning, she saw another useful person was coming. From a distance she raised her hand and with a broad smile cheered. "Hi, Madam Nightingale! It's a pleasure to see a benevolent lady like you." She introduced Dorothy. "She is Dorothy from Sri Lanka. Diana of course you know well. "Dorothy she is a world figure" She wanted to give a fair description as it would be useful to her when she returns to the Earth.

"During the Crimean war in Europe she volunteered as a nurse. Helped wounded people. Even at night she used to take lantern and visited wounded army people and treated them very kindly. That's how she came over here. She laid a foundation for a nursing school at St. Thomas hospital in London in 1880. She is one of the oldest here. Came on the 13th August, 1910."

"Thank you Marilyn for your long introduction for an old hand like me." She shook hand with Dorothy and sat on a velvet upholstered chair which was erupted for her when she was arriving.

"Although you are an old hand, you look like a lamissi." Dorothy uttered with a smile.

"What do you mean by lamissi? I have never heard that term earlier." Nightingale was inquisitive.

"Lamissi is a young woman in my Sinhala language. When a girl attained puberty, from that time onward, she will be known as lamissi until she gets married"

"After that she can't use that honorary term. She will lose it. Automatically! You are being a senior hand we can learn from you lot about heaven and earth."

"Heaven is an excellent sphere at the edge of the Milky way galaxy, although there are no greeneries. We have a healthy and pleasant atmosphere with perfumed smell although we haven't sprayed anything. No sun and moon but have constant day light. Not too hot not too cold. There is no one to annoy us. But other parts of the world are in utter chaos. Human beings are fighting each other on political reasons. In heaven there is absolutely no problem all are living happily as there are no male counterparts. And no politicians to mess up the heaven. No weapon manufacturers here to incite arrogant human beings to fight each other. So that they would be benefitted. No religions here which are all outdated. We need not pray any god or any devil. We have to just think, what we want. You get what you want. We are self-procreated.

Some define this as a physical or transcendental place. German called it Himmal. I presume it has derived from 'heben', that means to raise as heaven is always above. According to old English it is synonym with sky. Because primitive people thought shinning stars are gods. Their dwelling place is heaven. So sky became heaven. Whenever some think about god they always look up and sometimes pray. Any way this heaven is in the same galaxy as the Earth. Different languages, different religions give different names different definitions. But heaven is heaven, where there are full of joys. I have plenty of work to attend, Dorothy. When I got the news to say some one has arrived here before the death I got astonished and wanted to come and have a glance. Now another one from your country is on the way. Meet her and have a nice time. If you need anything tell our Supervisor Marilyn she will help you where ever necessary. There is a call from the King. I am off. Bye!"She left.

"You are…?"

"I am Lechchami, I was living in Chilaw. Married to a Sinhala business man. He is an owner of a tavern. He is having five hotels. Above all he is having an illicit gambling den. I had a love affair and got married to him although my parents raised objection. I have eight children. We have two women to do domestic work. But still he wants me to do all the work at home. Cooking, looking after children. Their schooling, Washing his clothes. When he goes to the well for bathing or washing I have to take him the towel and soap. He comes dead at night after hooch. Scold me for nothing. Dragged me, pushed me down, and raped me. Then sleep like a buffalo…"

"So, so, what happened, what happened?"

"I was chatting with our driver. Next door person who tried to approach me several times failed. On this he is having a grudge with me. He looked like a hawk on us and uttered, " ha-ha I'll tell your husband. You guys are trying to elope?"

"I scolded the fellow with filth."

Little while later my husband came in a hurry by a taxi. Scolded us in filth and said today is the last day you two dance and shot at both of us. Within a minute I came over here."

"You go to the king and explain to him clearly and then come back." Marilyn sent her to the king.

"There could have been something or due to ignorance got fed up with married life. If they had gone to see my Khajuraho, this would not have happened."Dorothy lamented.

Here comes a good friend of mine, popular movie

personality, Elizabeth Taylor. "Glad to meet you, all those who are beautiful, all those who have done a bit of honest job to please human beings, when they died they come over here. According to my book you had come on March 23,2011."

"Exactly correct. I am very happy here more than human world. Although throughout my human life I tried to please each and every one but I was not happy at the end. I had my first screen test when I was a tiny child, for the 'Gone with the wind'. Since then I was crazy for movies and I was in the field until my death. I had a very successful career."

"I can remember you in –'Can on a hot tin roof'. You were excellent."

"Yes I did my part in every movie pretty well. Got awards. But the tail end I was not happy."

"You know in Sri Lanka we had a very popular film star, by the name Eddie Jayamanna, they were living closer to our house in Negambo. His wife was the most popular film star in the island. Equally popular as a singer. They had a stage show, Broken Promise, in Nuwara Eliya. There was ample time for the show, so Eddie has come out for a loaf to see the town. There was a big Pharmacy. He has gone in and had asked the Pharmacist "Is there any medication to keep me happy.""

"Oh, my god you have suicidal thought. I too may have to give evidence. So far no such medication has been produced and researchers have absolutely no time to involve in research for such a medication. I'll tell you something. Today at the Town Hall there is a stage show where an Island famous comedian is taking part. He used to crack side splitting jokes! You go for the show. All your sad thinking will vanish. You will be extremely happy. Go and watch that. It is at 6.30.".

"It is a good news. Who is the comedian?"

"He is the most famous comedian, Eddie Jayamanna."
Eddie said, "Thank you," and he left."

"If you please others they will become happy. But you won't

become happy. You have to find other modes of entertainments to become happy."

"I have found other ways too. But still I was not happy. Only coming over here I am happy. This would be the eternal happiness to me. Excuse me guys. I am leaving. If any movie personality arrives here. Please inform me Marilyn. I am off." She left.

"The lady who went to the King is returning. Let us find out what has happened and will ask her how she ascended to heaven." Marilyn suggests.

"What did king said?"

He said it was a first degree murder and he will go to gallows. But that won't help me. Who will look after my innocent eight children?"

"What were the merits for you to come to heaven?" Dorothy asked.

"My husband arrives home after heavy booze. He brings lot of money may be from the gambling den. Both his jacket pockets are everyday brim full. He doesn't know how much there are. So I take lot of money to give ten poor Tamil families who have lost their husbands at the wretched war we had in Sri Lanka for 26 years. Those women do some casual work and earn a little. But that is not sufficient to feed their children. So daily I give 50 bucks to each family. I sent through my driver, other than that I absolutely no other bad connection with him. If he had shot me for taking money I can bare that. But killing me and that innocent fellow on completely wrong allegation that neighbour did. I am not agreeable and not happy."

"We understood you. You can be happy in the heaven. That your little charity helps you to come over here." Marilyn said and recorded her statement.

"You give me your name and address, I'll ask my husband to look into and I'll help the families you helped. I'll get a grant for them from the Government."

"Thank you."

She gave Marilyn her name and address and requested to give it to that good lady.

"Okay, you can go." Marilyn said.

If that miserable couple had the opportunity to watch my Art Gallery together they would have lead a happy life. I am quite sure."

"Now it is too late to think about the mishap. Let's advice future ascendants.

"Here comes a very popular figure in the recent history from your adjacent country."

She twisted her thumb and forefinger and made a sharp sound, at the very moment erupted a throne like comfortable chair, "Have a seat Mother Theresa."

"Thank you Marilyn, I never expected these comfort even when I was on the Earth."

"I know. But as we know you well we have to treat you with best we have."

"Reverend Mary said she also wanted to come over here to meet your guest who has come over here before her death."

"That's good. Now mother meet Dorothy. He is the wife of Religious Interests Minister in Sri Lanka."

"How glad to meet you Dorothy!" She shook hands. "Your three decade old terrorist troubles are now over. Your country people must be happy."

"Some are happy. Some are unhappy." She had a sigh.

"That is the nature on the Earth. If you do some good things to one party, there would be another party who got affected by your good work, who will become unhappy. Mostly contractors who provided various materials to those who engaged in war are now badly affected. Their revenue has become nil. So they are very unhappy."

"You can't please everyone. If the majority has become

happy you must content with that. That is more than enough. That is Democracy. I did so much of favorable work to people in India. But some people were quite against. Vishva Hindu Prasadh accused me that I am trying to proselytize people in India. They were against my stance of contraception and abortion. There were so many tiny tiny children in poor families. It was a big burden to them and children were suffering immensely. Marilyn you may have recorded my events. Why don't you illustrate to this lady."

"Moment." She turned her record book. "Mother Theresa came over here on 5th September 1997. She found the Missionaries of Charity in Calcutta, now called Kalkota, in 1950. For over 45 years she ministered to the poor, sick, orphaned, and dying.

She won the Noble Peace Prize in 1979. She opened a hospice Shanthi Nagar for the Leprosy patients and Nirmala Shishu Bavan for orphans and homeless children. Following her death she was beatified by Pope, John Paul the 11 and gave the title Blessed Theresa of Calcutta.

She was bestowed with the Padma Shree in 1962 and the Jawaharlal Nehru award for International understanding in 1969. In 1980 she was honoured with India's highest civilian award by the Indian Government, the Bharath Rathna award for humanitarian works.

"I got all the awards because they recognized my good work. Any way I didn't do any work expecting any reward. But it is a good thing to acknowledge the work I performed was beneficial. I am fully contented with that recognition. Marilyn see who is coming."

"Oh good gracious, Virgin Mary is coming."

"O, Don't address her as Virgin Mary. She doesn't like. She feels it as an insult to her."Florence, Marilyn and Dorothy got up and worshiped her. "Please take a seat Reverend Mary."

She sat on a cozy chair erupted for her at the very moment.

"I am very happy if you address me like that." She sat down and was eager to know about Dorothy who had ascended to heaven prior to her death.

Marilyn wanted to give an introduction on Dorothy. "She is the wife of Minister of Religious Interests in Sri Lanka who has undertaken a massive project-International Religious Complex, where replicas of most of the world famous Churches, Temples, Kovils and Mosques are to be built in one place."

"Oh, What a great bit of work, instead of going all over the world your country people venerate all these places with less expenditure."

"It is praiseworthy." Mother Theresa affirmed.

"So Dorothy as the wife of your great Minister you are not doing anything?"

"Why not?"

Marilyn started again. "She has started a Khajuraho. An Art Gallery with erotic art."

"Are you crazy Dorothy?"

"No Reverend Mary. There is a great significance in it. Most of the marriages of our people ended up in rock. If they know their husband and wife each other well. They sustain their intimacy without a break. They should know each other's mind and body equally well. If they could enjoy their sex life well and get the immense pleasure, they can sustain their lives well and could lead a happy life unto death. Sexual exploration is a lifelong process. My project will educate them, teach them better sexology and better living."

"Excellent Dorothy, excellent! What a beneficial project!"

"That's how she has come over to the heaven before her death." Marilyn affirmed.

"So you are going to be here permanently?"

"No, no." Marilyn interrupted.

"Unfortunately, only one hour. Virgin Mary. Sorry Reverend Mother Mary." Dorothy said.

"You know why I am personally not in favour of the term,

virgin. It sounded as an insult to a mother of a world figure. I am a mortal woman was living with my beloved husband although was not officially registered. Sexual intercourse is a biological need. There is nothing bad about it. Although according to various cultures having sex prior to marriage is a taboo. If they found wife, rather bride have had sex prior to marriage, husband and family members kick her out. It is prevailing in your country, isn't it?"

"Some times. Perhaps in remote villages. But in India and Pakistan, they are very strict."

"That is so." Mother Theresa confirmed.

"But now in those countries they have discovered a system. Hymen repair or re-virgination. It is a cosmetic surgery. Hymenoplasty. Doctors performed a surgery and made them virgin again. But they charged heavily. Only rich people could afford." Dorothy described.

"O, I see. Is it possible?" Mary exclaimed.

"But I am proud, that I was living with a husband and he is genuinely responsible for my baby. He is not illegitimate. Nobody needs not have any bad feeling and just sling mud at me and my husband. My baby became a religious leader in the wide world where millions and millions venerate him. I don't want be a virgin mother like Kunthi in Mahabaratha, where legend says she was a daughter of Suriya sun. Conceived by sun rays. There are several such mythological virgin births. Mine is no mythology. No magic or miracle. I delivered to the world a great religious leader."

"But those who didn't like him crucified him." Dorothy exclaimed.

"What is good to someone may not be good to another. That is the nature. But who believed him are living all over the world."

"With regard to the virgin concept, Marilyn opened up the subject again. "Now in advanced countries, with the female produced eggs, according to the system of 'parthenogenesis',

Doctors can develop an embryo in the womb without an intercourse, so that woman remain as a virgin." Marilyn described.

"Even so what is the pride a mother will have? Nonsense! Motherhood is not well recognized on the Earth. Mothers should be greatly cherished. Greatly admired. And particularly the mother of a great figure like Jesus Christ should be highly venerated." Reverend Mary sadly said.

This virgin business has created by Luke and Matthew. It may have been a pride for them. Therefore I do not want be harsh on them. In the NT L2 it describes, Emperor Augustus, ordered census to be taken, So we had to go to Bethlehem, It was King David's birth place, Joseph is a descendant of David, and I am his espoused wife. When we went there all the inns were full. I was pregnant, I was about to deliver the child. Immediately had to search for a place. We found a stable we forced to go there. I delivered my baby boy Jesus in that stable. Shepherds who came in the morning saw us and were very happy. They treated us very well according to their customs, when it comes to the registration of the child after one week, he has to be circumcised (L2:21) and named him as Jesus. About two years later, King Herods of Galilee had come to know from astrologers that a baby has born two years ago who will rule the whole world with his spirituality. This man got wild, he was a brutal king who had killed two of his children and wife. He had ordered to kill all those who are in that age range. Joseph was an intellectual and when he heard this he immediately made arrangement for us to flee. So that's how we escaped. Herods was ruling in 4BC to 6CE. Later when my boy was engaged in preaching and healing the sick and committed million good works, Jews who had a jealousy and fear arrested him and gave the judgment to crucify him. The two punishments that were prevailing for criminals, either to crucified or stone to death. He was subject to crucifixion. But he was not a criminal."

"So in return Jews didn't get any retaliation?"Dorothy asked.

"Hitler massacred 6 million of them in gas chambers without an iota of mercy." Marilyn said.

"These sooth Sayers, astrologers, palm readers and all these magicians play hell in our countries."Dorothy uttered.

"In heaven they can't perform all such magic or miracles here. When the heaven was creating I advised to build it up without sun moon and stars. Throughout the day we have the brightness here and the climate is always like this. Not too hot, neither cold. Now your Earth is rotating round the Sun, but here we can just see sun goes from one end of the sky and goes across to the other, as given in the Psalms 19.6.

But this has been marvelously built up, all the stars, moon and sun are below the heaven. One year on the earth is only one day in heaven. If you desire to eat anything, you just think about it, you get it. Anything is like that. Only happiness you have here. No worries. Beauty has got the prominence everywhere. But your case it would be different as you are a product of the Earth. It is very seldom politicians come over here, because they won't be recognized here. However some ascends. Now one of your Prime Ministers has come recently from some other planet. She is Srimavo Bandaranayke of Sri Lanka. I'll ask her to come and speak to you. I'll take your leave, bye!"

She disappeared. Your time is up Dorothy, unfortunately you have no time to meet her." Marilyn said.

"Thanks!"She uttered reluctantly and put on her filthy robe and asked, "Please Marilyn tell her that I am not fortunate enough to see her. Before leaving could I rush to the bath room?"

"No bath room, in the heaven. I told you earlier. We are not supposed to pollute the heaven."

"Then I am off, Merilyn. Bye, bye!"

"Bye, bye, Dorothy. I wish good luck to your Khajuraho!'"

"Thank you."

When Dorothy appeared in the ward of the Mental Hospital, the Matron yelled, "Where on earth you have been? We search all over, wanted to send radio messages to all the police stations in the island. Ultimately thinking that you are dead, we cut off you name from the Register…"

"Sorry madam, I went to the wash room."

"But, such a long time?"

"My constipation is terrible madam. Have to wait for a long time. Hours, days, months no limit."

"Okay, Okay now go and have your meals."

"Thank you madam!"

"Your name is Jane, Isn't it? We will re-enter."

Chapter 9
Sitha's Marriage and Revelation of Ramayana

After six months of the demise of Mrs. Senanayake, Guptha family with Mangala arrived as the Sitha's marriage has been fixed.

From the Airport Faizal accompanied them to Negambo Town to show them the New Bus Stand opened up last week. They highly appreciated the new complex. Immediately they arrived Doctor told the Minister, "Your Bus Stand is not seconded to any of the Omni-bus Stands in Europe, America or Canada."

"Yeah Doctor it is grand but these Marxist elements are criticizing whatever good we delivered. Recently we introduced luxury train services from Colombo to Kandy.Expo Rail and Rajadhani Express. Of course charges are high. These fellowes are protesting that we are trying to provide facilities only for the rich people."

"Well Minister that is the nature any where in the world. Worse in Third World countries. Must ignore Minister Must ignore and make every attempt to develop the country. Once the country is developed they will shut their mouths. In Canada 50 to 75 years back, car was a luxury. Now in every house there is one or two cars. It is not a luxury, it is a utility. Something essential. To reach necessary destination you need a comfortable car. You see it is the nature in any country for the opposition party elements to go against for any work carried out by the governing party. Just ignore!"

"Dogs bark at the moon! We can't stop that. President is adamant to build up a superb road net work, like in Canada. Now he is building up bridges wherever necessary, putting up fly over bridges in busy crossings. In five years time he will achieve his objectives." Minister divert his topic and requested them about their breakfast. They responded that they had at the flight and desired to have a nap prior to their planned trip to Nuwara Eliya.

Faizal and Sitha made necessary arrangement for them to have a nap.

Doctor and Sitha had a little bit of suspicion and desired to return the Style, whether that was a reason to the mysterious death of Mrs.Senanayake.

When Sitha expressed her notion on that Upasaka said Madam is not dead she is living, we have to search for her. Anyway if you wish you can return it but I have no power to go into the tunnel. You may have to do it by yourself. Let's try. Let's go there.

They wash their faces and hands. They walked in towards the cave. Upasaka stepped in and as usual lit a coconut lamp, burnt incense and camphor. Started reciting Sthothra. She got disappeared and returned in ten minutes. She said she had the opportunity to return it. When they came to the Upasaka's hut he looked at her hand and said that she will have to face a dangerous situation from a friendly enemy. So take great care.

Sitha is now attending Peradeniya Campus as a permanent Lecturer on Archaeology but avoiding any unwanted trips because of Upasaka's warning. Marriage of Sitha and Faizal was fixed to be taken as a minor ceremony in view of recent bereavement. Only few friends had been invited and fixed it as the official registration.

Day prior to her marriage Kumari has invited them for dinner at her house in Kandy as her parents are leaving on a pilgrimage to Lumbini on the day prior to her registration. So both of them agreed to visit. Kumari requested them to come prior to the departure of her parents in the afternoon. So they had to go early around four in the evening. Enjoyed thoroughly with wine and refreshments. Prior to the Dinner they emptied two bottles of wine.

"Don't take too much of liquor Faizal as you guys have to drive." Kumari's father advised.

"I thought Muslims do not take liquor." Mother said.

"I won't take much madam. By the time of dinner everything will be drained."

"Faizal is a modern Muslim. He won't adhere to Quran. Sitha said."

"Although he is a Muslim I too haven't noticed any attachment to his culture."

"I hate even the term culture. Unfit for the present era."

"Don't say so. We old people always cherish." Kumari's father remarks.

He didn't want to go against his view as he is strongly religious minded.

"In this changing world past things will become archaeology." Sitha argued.

"For her everything old is archaeology, because she is an archaeologist."Kumari remarked.

"Archaeologists know the value of anything old. Okay,

Okay, now we have to leave."Kumari's mother got ready to leave.

Kumari knelt down and venerated mother first and then the father.

They left in an auspicious time at 4.38, since then all the three enjoyed and had dinner around 10 at night. Kumari had applied in Sitha's wine glass a chemical so that following day she might get benumbed or paralyzed. After the dinner they kissed Kumari vigorously and said good night.

Kumari wished good bye and wished both of them a heavenly married life. Immediately they left she followed them by parent's car, hardy old Humber. It was about 12 midnight, less traffic. So they went fast. Kumari followed them in the same speed. At the top of the precipice of Kadugannawa she banged the car behind pretty hard. It went up the sky and toppled down to the valley. Kumari's car also had a high hop and dropped down with a blaze. Kumari at that time have repeated her Mantara. She was thrown off the car and dashed against a tree. Her left hand got severely cracked. Burn marks all over the face and the body has become disfigured. She got unconscious. Sitha and Faizal were thrown off. Faizal telephoned home and informed the accident. Minister, Doctor and Mrs.Guptha immediately came over. Minister had informed the Kadugannawa Police. Police arrived without delay. Sitha too was unconscious and leg was badly fractured at the ankle. They were taken to the Kadugannawa hospital. Following day morning Dr. Guptha has made arrangement to take her to Canada. All of them left in the morning by a Singaporean Airline to Toronto via Heathrow.

Kumari appeared little later at the Kandy hospital with a bogus complaint. After taking treatment following day she disappeared. Somehow or other having free meals from several kiosks and travelled by several buses free of charge approached Upasaka. She had to tell him the truth.

"I knew child. If you dig pits for others you are bound to have your own fall into it. Anyway, this is not your fault. You were the Kaikei in Ramayana, who hates Rama as she was adamant to send him to the forest and get the throne for her son. For that she was compelled to do lot of cruel things. You are Kaikei so you are committed to do things in the same manner. Fortunately because of the Mantra you can stay invisible where ever you want. I can cure you and lessen your pain. But mental agony would be there. You stay with me."

She was crying and agreed to stay with him as in this condition with disfigured face she can't go anywhere and face other people.

Sitha was admitted to a hospital, where the Orthopedist said leg has to be amputated. As she is a dancer he said he will do below the knee. Amputation is imperative to cure her completely. Doctor gave the permission for the surgery. Meanwhile as the Upasaka said Mrs. Senanayake is not dead. Doctor was inquisitive to check with his computer equipments.

She appeared but her outlook was completely different. However from her lips and certain features on the face Doctor was able to recognize her. When questioned where she is. She was bewildered and could not answer properly. She was not in good sense. Doctor was wandering whether she is under threat or died and incarnated. When he asked whether he can remember him. There was no answer. When she referred to Sitha's accident she just laughed. Doctor realized if she is living her mental faculty is completely out and decided to try out later.

However she conveyed the position to her wife and Sitha

as well as the Minister. But Minister was so sure that they cremated her body, as such there was no excitement.

Doctor didn't give up. He tried several days. But the response was not at all satisfactory. Ultimately gave up.

After a few weeks Orthopedist came to her bed. Asking about her condition, doctor said, "I had to amputate you above your knee, but when I learned you are a renowned dancer I thought twice and decided to do the surgery below the knee. Fortunately now it is quite all right. Fracture is almost set. But it has to get tightened. Mother Nature works with muscles and tendons to hold your ankle with metal and plastic to have a proper control for easy movements. In a few days time you may do the exercise and then under the supervision of an aerobic teacher you may keep your steps. Steps will sense the change in posture and weight distribution on your heel and change the level of resistance accurately. However courage, perseverance and unrelenting resolve you would be able to be successful in your dancing carrier. Wish you best of luck." Orthopedist wished her with a broad smile and left.

Wound got cured before three months. She had to walk with a prosthetic leg and get exercise under supervision for sometimes. Orthopedic trainer selected by the hospital trained her on steps and movements with the prosthetic leg. She got a thrill. She realized she can dance in the same manner as normal feet. Once she discharged an aerobic teacher came home and offered her methodical exercise suit for dancing, proper step movements etc. now she is absolutely normal. In six months time she was able to dance very well. She was keen to organize a show in Canada. Which she did. It was a success. Decided to go back to Sri Lanka with Faizal and invited parents to arrive soon for the wedding.

When she returned to Sri Lanka with the assistance of the Chithrasena Academy a show was organized. She first appeared, welcomed the crowd and described that she met with an accident, her leg was amputated (she showed the leg) and she dance today as an amputee with the prosthetic leg. It was a bit of amazement to the audience. Kumari was in the corner of the audience but was crying and was invisible. Minister and Chitrasena were in the first row and they too were really amazed.

She performed even a Bharatha Natyam with a strong ability. Her traditional Kandyan items, Ukusa and Giridevi dances had the usual stamina. Applause from the audience was so receptive.

Once the show was over when they were about to get into their vehicles Upasaka appeared. Congratulate Sitha and said he has to give happy news. "Mrs. Senanayake is not dead he is living. She was involved in a certain sinful activity behind the back of her husband for which she got a punishment. That will be over on the day Sitha is getting married. For her to appear on the day of the marriage a big tamasha has to be organized. I will appear with her at the right moment." Upasaka disappeared.

They were bewildering what should they do. When they came home the first thing Minister did was to dial the President and inform the unexpected revelation. He too got excited.

President suggests Minister to organize an Exhibition of a model of the Religious Complex in his premises on the day of the wedding and also if possible to arrange a dance recital where Sitha is performing for the public free of charge in the premises. Once the Dance Recital is over organize in that venue an Art Exhibition with all the Art works that Mrs. Senanayake has drawn. At the end of the Dance Show to fix the opening of the Exhibition followed by the registration of the marriage. Minister thanked him and agreed to arrange everything as he proposed and invited then and there to inaugurate the Exhibition and to attest on behalf of Sitha. He accepted the invitations.

Minister said no more discussions are necessary for this and suggests that everything will do according to President's suggestion.

They fixed a date then and there. Informed Dr. and Mrs. Guptha .Thereafter they started organizing all what they have to do. It was a big task. Massive undertaking. Following day morning Minister got in touch with several contractors and assigned all the major activities. Building up of a stage with a suitable open air theatre and the construction to house the Model of the International Religious Complex.

He got those who are engaged in the construction work at the Religious Complex to build up suitable replicas. Got in touch with Chithrasena and requested to organize the Dance Recital. Lighting is an extremely essential area. It was given over to two contractors. Cake was undertaken by the catering staff of the Parliament. Other activities, whatever necessary were the responsibilities of Sitha and Faizal. Several officers attached to the Ministry agreed to volunteer whatever the work assigned to them. When Iqbal learnt he immediately arrived at Minister's bungalow and discussed with them and undertook to initiate whatever he felt suitable for the occasion.

The Dance recital and Exhibition was publicized but they had a fear how to control the crowd. IGP assured he will attend to that and nothing to worry.

It was on the 1st of March and it was a Sunday. On the previous day Dr. Guptha, Mrs.Guptha, Mangala and Rudolf arrived. On the big day at 12.00 noon Upasaka visited and requested the Minister and Faizal. "As announced the Dance recital where Sitha is participating should start sharp at 7.00 p.m. Prior to that Mrs.Guptha, Mangala and Faizal should go to a place with Nelly your bionic bitch, to get released Mrs. Senanayake. Her outlook is bit different but Nelly could be identified. Her name there is not Senanayake but Jane. Hon Minister you may have to notify IGP to instruct authorities to release her. She should dress well and have make up before coming over here as there would be a big crowd. Expensive Sari and matching jewellery should be sent and on the way she should be taken to a beauty salon to dress herself well. She should present here at the opening of the Dance recital that is at 7.00. Immediately after the Dance show her Art Exhibition should be opened up…and he hushed…She is in the Mental Hospital. I will present here sharp at 8.00 pm. President arrives here at that moment to inaugurate the Exhibition. See you, bye!" He disappeared.

Around 5.00 pm crowd thronged to Temple Road. Several bus loads of police force were present well in advance. Glittering lights made the place a mini-heaven. Temple Road was closed for motor vehicles at 5.00pm. Only those who have valid passes were allowed. As scheduled Dance Recital will starts with a 'welcome dance' by Sitha and bevy of girls attached to Chithrasena Dance Academy. Recital has to go on till 8.00 pm. When it was over it was the rendezvous for the Art Exhibition which has been pre-arranged. All the art-works were ready behind the curtain.

As instructed Mrs.Guptha, Mangala and Faizal with Nelly went over to the Mental Hospital. The receptionist who has got the necessary orders, requested them to be seated until she comes. But Nelly entered went in and searched in several places and finally discovered. "Nelly, You have come here?" Dorothy got bewildered.

"Yes madam! We have come to accompany you home for Miss. Sitha and Mr. Faizal's wedding ceremony.

"How can I go to a wedding ceremony like this!"

Then came an attendant and wanted to accompany her to the Main counter. She got excited and immediately got dressed up what she was wearing when she was admitted to the Hospital. It was brought by the attendant.

She got surprised when she saw Faizal, Mrs.Guptha and Mangala.

"How can I go to a wedding like this?"

"Don't bother we have brought everything. On the way let's go to Moira's beauty salon for a change."

She agreed and thanked all the members of the staff for treating her well and left.

At the saloon she had make up and dressed up with a beautiful Sari and jewellery.

When she was coming didn't talk much but was thinking. Perhaps her mental faculty seems to be not quite normal. When arrived at home. She asked what is this place? It is like another heaven. Why there is such a big crowd?"

Faizal said, "There will be an exhibition of the International Religious Complex at 8.00 p.m. Now there will be a Dance Recital by Sitha and troupe of Chithrasena Dance Academy. There the Dance Recital is opening with Sitha's Namaste Dance item, just have a look madam…"

They watched it being in the car, but she was enthralled and wanted to watch it more. When Sitha's Namaste item was over they went in.

President who arrived to the Airport by a Helicopter, from there came over by the Limousine. When he stepped in Upasaka appeared and said "Here Sir, Mrs. Senanayake has come. He greeted her and sat down. But she talked something irrelevant. Little while later, Minister accompanied him to inaugurate the Exhibition of the Exact Modal of International Religious Complex. Mrs. Senanayake also followed them. President gave the scissor to her and asked to cut the ribbon. Somebody else immediately brought another scissor and handed over to the President. When both of them were cutting the ribbon bevy of girls starts singing a new National Anthem composed by the author of the story and arranged by Iqbal.

When it comes to an end a Massive fire work display organized by Iqbal was started. They came in and solemnized the wedding ceremony of Sitha and Faizal. President attested on behalf of Sitha and Iqbal for Faizal. Once it was over Upasaka announced Vibhisana and Sitha are reincarnated as engraved in the myth of Ramayana, and pointed out to Suraweera and his wife. These two are the real father and mother of Faizal. He is not a Muslim. He is a real Sinhalese. Son of a valiant couple!" Somebody was crying loud. But nobody was visible.

Faizal immediately knelt down and worshipped them. Sitha also followed. Sitha's father, Dr. Indrajith Das Guptha is the reincarnation of King Dasaratha of Ramayana. Sitha and Faizal knelt down and worshipped him.

Invisible Kumari who was seated besides Upasaka was crying. "Kaikei, the youngest queen of King Dasaratha who requested the King to send Rama to the forest in order to entrust the kingdom to her son, who is younger to Rama. She was a revengeful woman. She is responsible to amputate Sitha's leg. Kaikei, who incarnated as a daughter of an upcountry arrogant, aristocratic parents is repenting now. She is here badly disfigured and crying for what she did. But she is invisible as she has blessed with a Mantra of the mighty King of Lanka,

Ravana. I am reluctant to divulge her name at this moment but may I kindly request all of you to pardon her. I conclude my revelation and wish you all health, wealth and happiness." He disappeared. President too wished the new couple and left with his security staff. Fire work display is still going on. Temple road is still full of crowd. IGP ordered not to open the road enclosure until the crowd disperse. Mrs. Senanayake was apparently in a joyful mood. Iqbal came over and asked, "You don't like to see your Khajuraho?"

"Ah, Iqbal, I must go and see that. After all that is my venture!"

"Madam, there is a big crowd in the road. I am sure even the Khajuraho must be equally crowded with people poured over here. Let us go around mid-night. I'll accompany you. It is a full success as you envisaged.People are fully satisfied and thanking you for presenting such a venture for the sake of married people."

"Thank you Iqbal, thank you. Please come and pick me up. Invitees to the wedding and other well wishers who were around came over and greeted the wedded couple as well as Mrs. Senanayake.

Long firework display came to an end but still a massive crowd is in the road as the model Exhibition of the International Religious Complex is opened and the road is still closed for vehicles. As it was too late Mr.Iqbal came again and suggests, "Mrs. Senanayake, Let's visit Khajuraho tomorrow morning. With this crowd it is uncomfortable to go there. To be franked madam, it is a huge success! I'll see you in the morning. Good bye!"

She too greeted, "Good bye!"

THE END

(This book consists of American & UK English)

An Inspirational novel.

Foreword by Dr.Buddhdasa Bodhinayake.
The Therapy is a piquant love legend of an
inter- racial marriage originated in Sri Lanka
Developed in Maldives.Ended up in Canada.

It is persuasive!   Publisher-iUniverse,Inc.
                      1663 Liberty Drive
It is impressive!   Suite 300
                      Bloomington,
It is explosive!   1N 47403 -USA
                      Available on line
      e-mail - bk consultant- @iUniverse.com